Love, ISH

ALSO BY KAREN RIVERS

The Girl in the Well Is Me

love, ISH

KAREN RIVERS

DCB

Canada Council
for the Arts

Conseil des Arts
du Canada

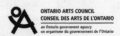

ONTARIO ARTS COUNCIL
CONSEIL DES ARTS DE L'ONTARIO
an Ontario government agency
un organisme du gouvernement de l'Ontario

Canadian   Patrimoine
Heritage   canadien

Canadä

The publisher gratefully acknowledges the support of the Canada Council for
the Arts and the Ontario Arts Council for its publishing program. We acknowl-
edge the financial support of the Government of Canada through the Canada
Book Fund (CBF) for our publishing activities, and the Government of Ontario
through the Ontario Media Development Corporation, an agency of the Ontario
Ministry of Culture, and the Ontario Book Publishing Tax Credit Program.

Library and Archives Canada Cataloguing in Publication

Rivers, Karen, 1970–, author
Love, Ish / Karen Rivers.

Issued in print and electronic formats.
ISBN 978-1-77086-492-4 (paperback). — ISBN 978-1-77086-493-1 (html)

I. Title.

PS8585.I8778L68 2017   jC813'.54   C2016-907288-6
                                             C2016-907289-4

Jacket design by Carla Weise
Jacket art © 2017 by Julie McLaughlin
Interior text design: Tannice Goddard, bookstopress.com
Printer: Friesens

Printed and bound in Canada.

Dancing Cat Books
An imprint of Cormorant Books Inc.
10 St. Mary Street, Suite 615, Toronto, Ontario, M4Y 1P9
www.dancingcatbooks.com
www.cormorantbooks.com

FOR LINDEN. WITH LOVE. I HOPE ONE DAY YOU GET TO MARS,
BUT I ALSO HOPE YOU NEVER LEAVE.

As a planet, the Earth is mostly OK, I guess. It's just not for me. You don't have to try to change my mind. It won't work! I know that there is plenty here that's terrific. But none of it is enough. Like, it's hard to argue against blue skies and puffy white clouds, fresh-cut lawns and cold, clear lakes, but these things are already on their way out. Thanks to global warming, the lawns are all dead and the lakes are drying up and the sky is polluted. We've wrecked it. Global warming is a real thing. You can pretend it's not, but that's just dumb. It's science.

There are still things that will make me ache inside from missing so much: ice cream, my parrot, Buzz Aldrin, and watching TV from the living room floor. I know that I'll lie on my bed in my dome, hearing nothing but the howling Mars wind, and I'll miss the silvery-shivery sound the wind makes in the trees when I'm lying on my bed at home, watching the shadows of those leaves moving around on my wall.

I'll miss jumping off our dock into the lake when the weather is really hot and the lake is cold (and not half-empty like it is right now because of the drought). It's the best feeling in the world. There aren't any lakes on Mars. Yet.

But even though I love Christmas mornings and piles of library books and the hammock that Dad strung up between the porch rail and the mailbox post and looking up at the stars at night, I'm still going to do it. I have to do it. It's what I was meant to do. I just know.

Most people don't get it, but in my mind, it's no different from what the explorers did when they came to America. They didn't know what they were in for. They definitely knew that they might not ever go home. So what's the diff? Someone has to be first, that's all. And if we don't spread out to other planets, the human race will eventually just die altogether.

Here's something you might not know: We are all made of stars. Up until last week, I just thought that was another poetic lie, like you see in the dentist's waiting room scrawled over a terrible painting of a night sky with the artsy-blurry kind of stars that make you feel like you need glasses. But according to Google, it's an actual fact: Every element on our whole planet — on all the planets — was created by imploding stars. People talk about how God created the world but really, the stars did. The stars are God. And we are stars. Think about it.

Why do we think that what we look like and what we wear matters at all, given that we're celestial? It doesn't! Who cares who you sit beside when you eat your sandwich at lunch? Why does it feel like it matters when

Amber Delgado laughs at you in gym class when you fall off the uneven bars and practically break your neck on the mat? Those are all just lies that our brains trick us into thinking are important so we don't remember that even though we're made of dead stars, we're alive, and one day, we're going to die, too.

I bet they just left the word *dead* off the poster and the coffee cup because death freaks people out. But everyone dies. What's the big deal? Life is a one-way trip for everyone. Right this second, your cells are slowly falling apart and you are that much closer to being dead, to being finished with your story. Don't you want yours to be amazing?

I do.

I don't believe those stars died so that we could have boring jobs so we can afford to buy a bunch of stuff that we later throw away, overflowing the landfills so bad that we have to leave the planet, which is exactly what's happening. It's already happened. Mars is the only option. Everywhere else is just too far. You might think that we can clean up the Earth and save the day, but no one is doing it. They are all just looking at their phones and complaining about the weather and not doing anything to undo the damage that's been done! It's a travesty.

And it's also why Mars is so important.

Everyone's scared, but not me. I'm ready. I was made for this. Mischa Love (Dead star #7,320,100,901), reporting for duty. I'm not going to waste this amazing, incredible life that the stars gave me. I'm going to be brave. I'm going to be special. I'm going to do what everyone else is scared to do.

And I'm going to be first in line to do it.

You'll see.

2

Mom thinks that I'll grow out of it one day and decide that instead of being a Martian settler, I'll eventually choose to be someone normal, like a teacher or a doctor. Well, she's nuts and she's wrong. When I see pictures of Mars, it looks like home to me, much more than our split-level, four-bedroom house on the water in Lake Ochoa, California. Mars is my destiny, if you believe in stuff like love and Fate. (I don't give two beans about love, but Fate is the real thing. I know it is.)

Even if I die on Mars (or on the way to Mars), at least I'll have tried. If you aren't trying, all those stars died for no reason! And that's tragic! They sure didn't go through all that compressing and colliding and imploding and creating so that we can buy new Converse high-tops at the Lake Ochoa Mall, which is what we are doing right this minute, even though my old Converse high-tops are perfectly fine. If you're keeping track, my feet are still a woman's size 6. I choose black ones, even though Mom is going berserk over the pink.

"If you like them, you should get them for yourself," I suggest.

"But I don't like them for me," she says. "I like them for you. They're fun."

"Mom," I say. "I'm not fun."

"OK" she says, looking sad. "We'll take these." Mom has a way of saying some things so that it sounds like one huge exhalation, a sentence made from a sigh.

"Sorry!" I say. "I just can't . . . pink."

She smiles at me. "I know." She pokes her pointer finger against the end of my nose and I duck. I'm too old for that. Seriously.

The salesman wraps the black shoes in tissue before putting them back in the box, like they are precious glass ornaments and not just regular sneakers.

I roll my eyes. I hate packaging. All that waste! "We don't need the box," I murmur.

"Pardon?" he says.

"Mischa," Mom says, with a warning in her voice.

"What?" I say. "I didn't say anything."

"I'll meet you out front," she tells me. "I'll just pay."

I wasn't going to tell him about the island of plastic floating around the Pacific Ocean, killing seabirds and whales! I just didn't want the box!

I wander out to the front of the store and wait, leaning on a fake plant's huge pot. I wonder who the first person was to think, "Hey, real plants are a lot of trouble, let's make plastic ones." The whole world is the laziest. Period. One day this terrible plastic plant will get thrown away and it will never disintegrate. This ugly thing is eternal. It hurts my stomach, just thinking about it.

People are wandering by, looking at their phones, typing with their thumbs. Hardly anyone ever looks up. What is so important that they can't even get from Taco Bell to Old Navy without typing something? More points in favor of Mars: There won't be cell phones. There won't be cell towers. And no one will care if you have the iPhone 42 or not.

The only bad thing is that missions won't be leaving for at least ten years. In the meantime, the Mars Now website says they are sending up supplies so that by then, everything we need will be there. Biomes and food supplies and equipment and vehicles and everything like that. (If you don't know, biomes are the gardens that we'll grow inside geodesic domes on Mars, protected from the elements. The biomes are in domes so that when storms blow, the wind doesn't tear them apart. The wind just slips off round things. It can't fill them up like sails, lift them up and destroy them.)

We will have plenty of biomes on Mars. (And storms.) Maybe a dome for each of us, like houses of our own. A whole neighborhood of biomes. Can you even imagine? It will be so amazing.

But what they'll need most of all on Mars is young people. People like me are going to be important soon, no matter how unimportant I am right now, shopping with my mom for stuff I don't want while unmanned missions are filling a crater that Mars Now has named

New America with everything we'll need to survive, to start over.

In ten years, I'll be twenty-two. It doesn't sound that old. I mean, it's old but not ancient, not Mom-aged, not dying. And if you think about it (and if the organizers think about it), twenty-two is the perfect age: Young. Healthy. Strong. My frontal lobe will have finished developing and I'll basically be the smartest that I'll ever be in my whole life. (After your early twenties, it's all downhill. That's just science.)

I know that I can convince them. I have to convince them! I *will* convince them.

My heart races with excitement just thinking about it. I take a deep breath and lean slightly onto this hideous plantlike thing, grinning like a weirdo.

I'll probably be famous back here on Earth. People will say, "Mischa Love was the first girl on Mars. Mischa Love was the one who paved the way. Mischa Love changed everything." And I won't even know, because I'll be busy surviving, making a new world for people to live in. If that isn't exciting, I don't know what is! (Hint: definitely not a fifty-percent-off at Forever 21.)

On Mars, no one will care about back-to-school fashions. On Mars, there are no malls. There's survival. And that's it. I don't understand why everyone doesn't want to go to Mars, to start over, to never shop again.

"If you move to Mars, won't you miss this?" Mom says now, coming out of the store and handing me the bag, gesturing at a crowd of people sitting around the food court, stuffing Cinnabons into their pieholes as though there is nowhere else they would like to be.

"No," I answer, very honestly. "I definitely won't."

The mall air is so terrible that even my eyes feel dry. When I blink, my eyelids make little *tick,tick,tick* sounds. I do it a few times in a row because I can't tell if it's a feeling or just a sound. "Can you hear this?" I ask Mom, blinking extra hard.

"What about your friends?" she asks, ignoring the question. "Won't you miss them? Want a Cinnabon?"

"Are you saying *friends* with ironic air quotes?" I ask. "And no. Cinnabon is gross. Empty calories." I believe in eating what you need to eat to survive and not a bunch of chemicals disguised as food. Mom knows this! If my body gets used to eating sugar and fat, then Mars will be very hard for me. There aren't any fast-food outlets there. We'll mostly be eating easy-to-grow, fast crops, like potatoes and root vegetables and whatever else is going to thrive in our biomes. And, of course, freeze-dried things and protein packs, at least for a little while. I can't be a fussy eater on the ship we take to get there, either. There's no room for that.

"No," she says. "I don't use ironic air quotes. I meant, 'the kids in your class, who you sometimes socialize with.'" She makes ironic air quotes with her fingers around "the kids in your class" and smiles, to let me know she's being funny.

"Then definitely not," I say, not giving her a laugh. "One hundred percent, for sure, no."

"I like Cinnabons," she says, wistfully.

"Mom," I say. "Ugh."

"Fine," she says. "OK, you're right."

We stand there for a minute, just watching the people ebbing and flowing and chewing and swallowing and spending money on credit so they can own a pair of jeans that go in at the bottom instead of out, or whatever the random Jeans Rules are this year. I close my eyes. These are definitely not my people! Why are most people not my people?

Here is the most important thing you can know about me: Tig Diaz was my people. My only person. My one-and-only-forever-friend.

And now he's not just gone, he's DTM (Dead To Me) for *reasons*, not the least of which is that he moved to Portland last year and never once answered any of my messages. I guess that after he got there, he decided to be someone new, someone whose best friend wasn't the weirdo-girl-next-door. And just like that, "forever" and "I promise" were done and dusted, blown into the past in a whoosh of wind and rain.

His new friends are probably all boys, tough and wild, who hurtle on their BMXs down ramps at bike parks, their knees scratched and bleeding, grinning from ear to ear in that dumb, vacant way that only sporty boys have. I bet they don't care about Mars. Probably Tig has stopped fainting at the sight of blood. Maybe he can ride like a champ now, bouncing off those jumps like he's flying, white teeth gleaming in the sun, not scared to death about what happens if he falls.

The thing is that he promised — we promised — that we'd never leave each other behind, alone, to fend for ourselves. Not on Mars. Not anywhere.

And he lied.

So, like I said, DTM.

Get it? Got it?

Good.

3

Applying to go to Mars was Tig's idea in the first place. He fell in love with Mars before I did.

We talked for six whole years about what it will be like when we finally go. Tig had journals filled with pages and pages of our plans, what we could grow, how we'd survive if we got left behind like that guy in that movie. Left for dead. How we'd be able to figure it out and keep going, all written out in his tiny, perfect handwriting. Boys are supposed to have messy writing, but that was just one of the billion ways that he was different from everyone else.

Different and better.

Sometimes he'd call me in the middle of the night on the landline that Mom and Dad let me have installed in my room, as a compromise, because I needed to be able to communicate but they didn't want me having a cell phone. Not yet. Anyway, I'd keep the ringer on low and sleep with it under my pillow. Almost every other night, he'd have an idea, and my phone would ring soft and low and I'd answer it and there he'd be, in the middle of a sentence about how to leach the perchlorate (which is toxic to humans) out of the Mars dirt using this one kind of bacteria that eats it. Or he'd be like, "If the outer layer of the biome is shattered by blowing dust, the inner layer should be made to push outward while robots build another inner layer. But I guess the biome would get smaller and smaller. I've got to go. I gotta think about that some more. Bye, Ish."

He always said good-bye. Right up until he didn't.

Now I don't know if he's even still sending applications to Mars Now. His old house has been empty for nine months, four days, and sixteen hours. The FOR SALE sign, which I can see from my bedroom window, went crooked in the last windstorm and no one has righted it. Even the realtor must know that it's hopeless. No one moves to Lake Ochoa. Not since the factory on the other side of the lake spilled a bunch of chemicals into the water that made the lake turn bright blue-green. It looked beautiful, like a postcard, but it turned out it was poison.

It's better now, that's what they say. They did tests and the water is plain old water, it's just that nothing lives in it anymore. Tig says that we can bet it's full of perchlorates that they aren't telling us about, that they are everywhere here because humans have made a mess of things and pretty soon we'll have the same problem as Mars does: water, but none we can drink. But Dad says he's wrong, that the tests have come back clean. I never know who to believe. Either way, I can see how that doesn't look good to people coming in from out of town. They just keep on heading down the highway to bigger and better lakes, lakes without beautiful toxic sludge, normal gray lakes with trout swimming in them, with water-skiers and good futures.

The front grass at Tig's old house is as high as my knees and full of angry-looking weeds, spiked with thorns. I admire weeds. Weeds are what grow when nothing else will. Weeds have an enthusiasm that prettier plants can't be bothered with! If people were all either flowers or weeds, I'd be a weed. Weeds are survivors. Weeds are what they need on Mars. Nothing fragile. No one who will die at the first sign of trouble. But still, the Diazes' old lawn doesn't look very good. The place looks abandoned (which it is), and a jaggedy crack has formed above the front door and goes all the way up to Tig's old bedroom window.

"I know how you feel," I tell that yellow house every time I ride by on my bike. If people broke when their hearts did, I'd have a crack just like that from my forehead to my feet, that's how bad I miss Tig. Instead, I've just decided that my heart is officially closed for business. Locked up for good. Love just gets in the way of what matters! (Even if it's not love-love, just friend-love, which is a totally different thing.)

What matters is Mars. Mars is the way we're going to survive! Earth is broken. We aren't weeds. We won't survive it.

"Oh, look," Mom says, startling me. "A sale on those cute sweaters!"

The way she says *cute* makes me cringe. "Cuuuuuu-uuute," with the *u*'s all drawn out like that, in a swoop of violin-string vowels. All the girls at my school talk like that, but when I do it, it sounds like I'm pretending to be someone else, which I guess I am. Don't get me wrong, I don't hate those girls or anything. They're fine, but they're just so *girly*. I don't get them. Which is fair because they don't get me, either.

"I have enough clothes!" I tell her. "This is plenty." So far, Mom has bought me three pairs of jeans (that go in at the bottom so tight I can hardly jam my foot through them) and sixteen white T-shirts (eight short-sleeved, eight long-sleeved). I only ever wear jeans and white T-shirts except in the summer when I wear jean shorts and white tank tops. I also have an orange Gore-Tex jacket that I wear over everything. It makes me look like I work for NASA, which I might one day, although the private missions are better for a bunch of reasons. But I'll take what I can get! (It's a great jacket. It has lots of pockets.)

Mom holds up a bright green sweater in front of me, pressing it into my chest like I should want to reach out and hug it. It is the worst. A twirling pattern of sparkling buttons glitters down the front of it, like a Disney princess threw up. Mom has obviously mistaken me for an ice dancer or a regular girl who is going into seventh grade at Teddy Roosevelt Middle School.

I'm not a regular girl.

"Mom," I say. "No."

"It's fun to try something different," she says. "It really is. And this green looks amazing with your hair."

"No way," I say, firmly. I think there is some law that states that if you have red hair, it's necessary for you to always wear green and look like a leprechaun. I refuse to bow to this pressure! I pick up a gray hoodie instead and rub the inside of it with my thumb. It's soft, like an old blanket.

"This?" Mom says. "Ugh. It's so boyish, though. It's plain! Don't you want to feel pretty?"

"It's nice," I say. "It's great! Feel it." I rub the fabric against her cheek.

She looks dubious.

"Please," I say. "I really love it."

"OK," Mom says. "Fine." She looks sadly at the green sweater. "Are you sure?"

"*Mom,*" I say.

She sighs and takes the hoodie up to the register to pay. I'm standing there thinking about how long it will take Mars to evolve to become a giant intergalactic shopping mall when I hear them. *Them.*

Nooooo.

I duck behind a rack of colorful jean jackets and pretend to tie my shoe, but I'm wearing flip-flops, so I just crouch there and fiddle with them a little. "Act natural," I whisper to myself. The skin on the top of my toes is tanned and there is a white stripe where the flip-flop strap goes. My feet aren't very clean.

The gaggle of girls swarms by, buzzing like bees on a mission. I do not know anyone who giggles as much as the twelve-year-old girls in my class. Sometimes I think I was programmed wrong at the factory. I mean, I just don't find anything as funny as they find everything. The girls stop. I'm basically trapped. I can't stay down here forever, so I stand up, reluctantly.

The girls are smiling and drinking Orange Juliuses and touching their hair. They do that a lot. Their hands are always twiddling. Why? They hover outside the entrance to the store and because I am unlucky and also brightly colored (see: red hair), they spot me. (In nature, red means "stay away! danger!" I wish it also worked that way in malls.)

The girls wave with the enthusiasm that you can only muster up when you are so used to faking everything that you don't know when you are faking it or if you really mean it anymore. In case Mom is watching, I make myself greet them: "Oh, hi, Ashley, Ana Sofia, Camilla, Bea," I rattle off their names like it's roll call, plastering a smile on my face. "Zoe, Amber, Alex, Kaitlyn."

"OMG, hiiiiiiiiiii," they answer, "Hi hi hi hi hi hiiiiiiiiiii Miiiiiischa!" They seem a lot happier to see me than I am to see them. Then, like a single organism, they swivel back into a closed circle, heads tipped, hips cocked, whispering.

I leave the store. Fast.

"Ish," Mom calls after me in a singsongy-and-loud-enough-for-them-to-hear Mom-voice. "Do you want to stay and hang out with your friends? I can pick you up later!"

"No," I say, over my shoulder. "No, thank you." I pick up my pace, practically running to the doors, heavy bags of back-to-school clothes and paper and pens and glue sticks and pencils banging against my legs. Once I get outside, I break into a sprint. I beat Mom to our car by almost three and a half whole minutes, the sun glaring down on my sweaty nose, turning it redder and more freckly than ever. It sucks to be a redhead in summer, trust me. (And it's no cakewalk the rest of the year, either, unless you like random strangers patting you on the head and going, "Oooooooh, I love your hair." Which I do not. I'm thinking about shaving my head. It would be very practical! There won't be shampoo on Mars.)

"You know," pants Mom, finally catching up, "you should give them a chance. If you got to know them, you might like them."

"I've given them lots of chances," I say, scowling. "I know them fine!"

"Maybe you should try to just . . ."

"Just what, Mom? Be like them? Pretend to like them?"

"Never mind," she says, starting the engine. "I was going to say, 'Maybe you should just lighten up,' but you know what? You have to figure this stuff out for yourself."

"Whatever," I say. "There's no law that says you're totally required to have friends in middle school. I like being alone. I'm a loner. It's better for my psychological profile to show that I don't need a bunch of people around me all the time."

"You've always had Tig," she says. "I know you miss him. But you can't just go it alone forevermore now."

"DTM," I remind her. "Dead To Me. Don't say that name. Not ever. Not even once more." Then I add, "And no one says 'forevermore,' Mom. This is not 1898."

"Ish," she says. She takes a big huge breath, like a massive speech is about to follow, but then she just says, "I'm sorry."

I shrug and turn the radio on. A sappy song from the eighties leaks out all over the car, filling up our silence with gooey lies about love. Love is a bill of goods that's been sold to us by savvy marketers. Think about all the stuff that love sells! Heart-shaped jewelry, for one thing. Red roses. You know, all that junk.

Mom sings along. She knows every word to every song ever, but she sometimes loses the car in the parking lot. Her brain-workings are a mystery. For example, when she was my age, she had to memorize the poem "Jabberwocky," including all the punctuation. She still remembers it. Every comma, every everything. When I was little and I couldn't sleep, she'd sit on the edge of my bed and recite the whole thing. "Apostrophe Twas brillig comma and the slithy toves carriage return Did gyre and gimble in the wabe colon carriage return All mimsy were the borogoves comma carriage return And the mome raths outgrabe period," she'd recite. It sounds weird, but I found it pretty soothing. (If you don't know, "carriage return" has to do with when you are typing on an actual typewriter. My mom is quite old. Obviously if we had to do that now, we'd say "enter," but it sounds prettier her way.)

I roll my window down as we pass through the mostly closed-up downtown, which is only four blocks long. The air is holding on to the wet, greenish smell of the lake all mixed in with the hot pavement of the road and the dryness of everything. All the good shops moved to the behemoth air-conditioned mall when it opened, leaving hot, shadowy spaces behind, like words censored from a sentence. Some of the empty stores have broken windows. They are almost all covered in graffiti. I wish the graffiti artists spent more time making nice paintings instead of just spraying swears, or at least, if they're going to do swears, spell them right. How hard is it to spell a four-letter word?

What's left unscathed are the stores that are still open: the post office, the bail bondsman, the pawn shop, the store that sells beer and cigarettes, and a used-book store that no one ever goes into, ever. Dad says it is probably a cover operation for a drug cartel. (If that were the case, you'd think they'd invest in a proper sign, not just a handwritten cardboard one that says BOOKS 50 CENTS. But on the plus side, they spelled it right!)

Dad is a screenwriter, so he has a crazy imagination. He writes animated movies. Well, he's one person of a billion who write those scripts as a team. His super-specific job is to punch the script up with jokes. That's the actual word: *punch*. His job title is "punch doctor." It says that right on his business card, above a pencil sketch of a hand curled into a fist. He's trying to work the used-book store/drug cartel into the film he's working on right now, which is about cute pale-pink Martians who land on Earth by mistake. I am deeply offended by the inaccurate portrayal of Martians, who — if they exist (which continues to be very unlikely) — are just bacteria, at best. But Dad tells me to lighten up, buttercup. If you ask me, Dad is too light. I'm surprised he doesn't float right off into space sometimes, that's how light he is.

(That was a joke, in case you didn't notice. I'm not very good at jokes, but I'm trying. Everyone gets better at everything if they practice it.)

Every other shop on this street has a big FOR SALE OR LEASE sign in the window, even the old ice cream shop. I miss that one the most. We used to go there every Sunday for family outings before Iris moved away. We rode our bikes. The last cone I had there had a dead fly stuck into the pointy part at the bottom and I only noticed it at the last second before I popped the whole thing into my mouth. I haven't eaten a cone since. That last one gave me the ongoing gift of cone phobia.

"Thanks for nothing," I tell the shuttered shop as we pass. "I miss you." The hot wind snatches my words and throws them onto the deserted sidewalk, where they turn into tumbleweeds and tumble away, like in an old Western story.

"What?" Mom says.

"Nothing," I tell her. "Don't let me interrupt your lovely song."

The song ends on a long drawn-out youuuuuuuuuu-uuuuuuuuu and then Mom barely even takes a breath before she launches right into her favorite topic of conversation, which is How To Have More Friends And Why It Matters. This includes such gems as "give it time" and "they just don't know you very well" and "one-on-one they might be less overwhelming" and "do you want me to get you a playdate with _____" and "the friends you make now are your friends for life."

"Mom," I interrupt. "We're almost thirteen years old. No one does 'playdates' anymore."

"I was just checking to see if you were listening," she says.

"I'm listening," I half-lie.

We slow down as we go past the playground where Tig and I built a tree house two summers ago. It wasn't very good. It fell down earlier this month. I think it was hit by lightning. It tipped right over and dumped itself, our two chairs, and my copy of the classic novel *The Martian* into the shrubbery. Parts of the structure are still sticking up out of the blackberry bramble. One day, I'll risk being scratched to bits to rescue the book, at least. Or maybe I'll go to the drug cartel's bookshop and buy another one for fifty cents. That old one is probably pretty moldy and gross by now. Or maybe it's been eaten by a squirrel. Squirrels will eat anything. Once they ate through all the wiring in our attic and started a fire that burned a perfect circle in our roof. You can still see it because the roofing stuff is newer in just that one spot.

While we wait for the light to change, I wave my pinkie finger at the place where the tree house used to be. Tig and I invented the finger wave so we could communicate at school without actually talking to each other. It was pretty important to us that no one knew we were friends outside of school because he is a boy and I am a girl and people would think something that wasn't true if they knew we loved each other. We decided on the first day of kindergarten. I don't remember why we kept doing it all the way through the end of fifth grade, because by then everyone knew we were BFFs. I know they knew because in the third stall in the downstairs bathroom someone wrote "Ish loves Tig" and someone else wrote "They are just friends, you jerk" underneath. I'm not saying who wrote the second part, but it was written in red Sharpie and I always have one of those in my pocket, just in case someone has misspelled something on a wall and it needs correcting. You'd be surprised how often people use apostrophes where they shouldn't, like in "nacho's" or "pizza's." There is almost never a time when a nacho or a pizza owns something! I mean, come on.

Mom is at the part of her speech where she is reiterating how important it is to give the girls a chance — as though they are all desperate to have me as a friend, ha — and that it will take time and that people change or that, wait, actually, *Maybe* I won't find my people until I grow up, and that's OK, too, as long as I stay open to the Universe and the possibility that my future BFF is someone I already know but haven't noticed yet. Then she says that it's possible that in a small town like Lake Ochoa, I'm just misunderstood.

I wait for a beat so that the silence filling the car can contain everything I'm thinking, which is, *You don't understand anything.* Then I say, "Like monsters and bad guys always are in Dad's movies? Scary-looking! But hearts of gold, am I right?"

"Ha-ha," she says. "Very funny. But yes. Sort of. You know, I didn't find my people until I went to college. Then as soon as I met them, I knew. Oh, there you are, I felt like saying. Where have you been?"

"Martians are my people," I tell her. "Will be my people, I mean. When I go."

"You're not a Martian, honey," she says. "You're just

too intense for these kids right now, but they'll catch up eventually. You'll see."

"But Mom," I say. "Once I move there, I will be a Martian, just like people from Canada are Canadians. Right?"

"But if you moved to Canada, you wouldn't be Canadian," she said. "You'd be an expat who happened to live in Canada. Unless you renounced your US citizenship. Which, I suppose, you could — "

"Fine," I say. "My people will be expats who happen to live on Mars."

"Right," she says. "OK. You win. Just promise me that before you go, you'll at least try college for a while, just to see if you might find someone or something a little closer to home."

"Mom," I say. "I'm going to Mars and you can't stop me. It's not going to be for a decade. Stop freaking out. I'll go to college! I'll do everything. I'm sure I'll have new friends this year. Whatever. I don't care! It's fine! I'm fine! Everything is fine!" A headache starts pushing down on my brain. I push it back. It pushes harder. I close my eyes and wait for it to pass.

Mom doesn't think I'll be picked for any of the manned Mars stuff, I know she doesn't. It doesn't feel very good to have a mom who doesn't believe in your dreams, let me tell you that. This is America! Anyone can do anything! Hasn't she paid attention to the message hidden inside every movie and every book ever?

NOTHING IS IMPOSSIBLE! Cue theme music! And optimism!

The trouble is that at this rate, she's right. Mars Now seems pretty busy promoting their reality TV show and taking photos of the already chosen participants in bathing suits with their muscles rippling, their hair shimmering in the sun. It's pretty dumb because on Mars, looks are the last things that will matter. Being smart and strong will be the things that count! I've been lifting weights in the garage with Dad and going for long runs around the lake so that I can be as fit as anyone by the time my turn comes. My biceps pop up like oranges under my skin when I flex my arms; when I run, my legs ripple like the legs of a horse pounding down the track.

"I'm a machine," I whisper to myself. "My body is a machine." It makes me feel better to think that way. Machines don't have feelings. Machines don't have hearts or hopes or dreams. Machines don't feel stupidly lonely when their best friend leaves town. They don't have seventh grade, looming on the horizon, replete with a new middle school and giggling girls who they don't know how to understand. They definitely don't get headaches.

Mom starts singing along to another song, loud and off-key.

"I miss you, Tig," I whisper out the window, and this time, my words aren't even strong enough to get blown out of the car, they just plop on the floor with the old straw-wrappers and shoe-dirt. They lie there beside my dirty summer feet, like there isn't anywhere for them to go, even if they could.

4

Mom pulls into the driveway in a cloud of brownish-gray dust. Everything is dry, dry, dry. It's the driest dry in the world, in the history of time. Drier than the desert, even. Drier than Mars. It hasn't rained for weeks or maybe actually months, I forget when the drought started, exactly. Now the lake — which wasn't very big to begin with — is sinking away from its beaches, leaving dry, cracked mud around the edge that looks a lot like Mars, actually. I like to sit on it and trace the cracks with my fingers, all those crevices reaching as deep as they can, thirsty for water to fill them up. It's my Mars, but I know it really isn't. If Tig were still here, we could pretend, though. We would pretend. Tig didn't think pretending was dumb. Tig wouldn't have rolled his eyes or laughed. But Tig is DTM!

Anyway, this is nothing like Mars. Mars is freezing cold. Too cold, really. (Things I will miss/TIWM: the hot smell of Earth summer. Things I will not miss/TIWNM: mosquitoes, heat waves, missing Tig.) But if I'm going to Mars, I have to get used to droughts. Even though NASA found flowing water, it's not a lot. It's not *lakes*.

It's more like marks on the ground, the mostly empty veins of something that used to flow.

Dad's bike is leaning up against the fence, so he's home. He rides twenty miles a day, just because.

"Because he's *procrastinating*," Mom always says.

"Am not," Dad always replies. "It helps me think! I have my best ideas on the bike!"

I think the truth is that he just likes how it feels to have the road spinning away under his tires, his legs pumping and carrying him faster and faster and faster. I like it, too. I get it. I'll miss bike riding when I'm on Mars. I'll miss Dad, too. Sometimes I get stuck thinking about all that I'll miss and I feel like crying, but it won't stop me from going. Nothing will. It's too important.

The lawn mower is parked in the middle of the mostly dead lawn like someone (Elliott) got bored halfway through and wandered off. Elliott is fourteen, almost fifteen. She is beautiful, which is the major thing you need to know about her. Her beauty is so shocking that people sometimes gasp when they see her, or at least do a double take. It's like her edges were drawn more sharply than other people's, and next to her, everyone else looks blurry. And she doesn't even try, believe me. She also has ADD and a whole boatload of other issues, meaning that what Mom says next is pretty typical.

"Oh, great!" Mom says, happily. "Ell started to mow the lawn!"

I mean, a more normal response might be, "Why can't

that kid ever finish what she starts?" But ours is not a normal family. Iris — my oldest sister — is the only normal one and she's at college in New York. She's going to be a fashion designer. I don't care about clothes, but even I can tell that hers are really really cool. Iris is kind and normal-pretty and smart and popular and super nice and talented. She's everything a parent could ever want. She's a dream daughter. Why my parents didn't stop after Iris is a real mystery. They ended up with a bully and a geek. How lucky! Being a trailblazing Mars settler is the least I can do to justify their choice of me, I suppose.

The main difference between Iris and Elliott is that Iris is happy to be pretty and happy to be smart and happy to be kind and just generally happy, whereas Elliott is *furious* that she was born beautiful and does everything she can to fight it (she recently shaved off her eyebrows and dyed her hair gray), which (ironically!) only makes her prettier. I'd feel sorry for her if I didn't hate her a lot, which I do most of the time. Living with Elliott is sort of like coexisting with a talking, breathing shard of broken glass. You never know when it's going to poke you in the foot and leave you bleeding all over the clean floor.

I help Mom with the shopping bags and then I take my usual spot at the kitchen counter with my laptop while Mom starts making dinner. In the corner of the kitchen, Buzz Aldrin says, "Rabbit, rabbit, rabbit." A long time ago, I tried to teach him to ribbit like a frog, but he never quite got it right. We used to have a lot of frogs here. The frogs are all gone now. I don't know what's happened to them. I suppose they left when the lake went bad. Left or died. "Rabbit," Buzz Aldrin says again.

Buzz Aldrin is an albino, which means he has no pigment. He is white, with red eyes, which is every bit as creepy as it sounds. When I was little and my Grandpa Hoppy (he lost a leg in the war) gave him to me, I thought he was a ghost! I mean, he looked pretty dead. I was screaming-and-running-away-level scared. He's grown on me now, though. It's not his fault that he's got terrifying eyes, any more than it's my fault that I have red hair and freckles that look like I stood too close to a can of spray paint. It's probably for the best that you can't take your freaky albino parrot to Mars in your carry-on bag. Nine months of having to listen to him saying "Rabbit" would do anyone in.

"Ribbit," I say to him. "It's *rib*-bit."

"Ten-four, roger, duck," Buzz Aldrin says.

I don't know how old Buzz was when Grandpa Hoppy bought him, but I'm guessing he was already retired from his job and starting to develop a serious relationship with his favorite TV game shows. Buzz Aldrin's feathers are patchy and his eyes are cloudy with time and tiredness. He likes to hang upside down in the cage and flap his wings, little bits of feather puffing out of the cage in the storm, but he never flies. I don't think he remembers how. When he blinks, the papery bird-skin around his eyes wrinkles and shivers.

"One small step," Buzz Aldrin says sadly. "One small step."

"Shhh," I tell him. "It's OK."

"Rabbit," he says, and climbs back onto his swing so he can stare out the window.

I wonder if Buzz Aldrin wishes he could go outside. I wonder if he dreams of leaving, just like me. I wonder if he imagines escaping somehow and taking off, flying higher and higher until he's gone. I would, if I were a bird.

"Houston," he says. "We have a problem."

I go to the Mars Now website, but nothing has changed since the last time I looked. It still says "Accepting applications, all ages considered."

Liars. "You sit on a throne of lies!" I tell the screen. That's from my favorite movie, which is *Elf*.

"What?" Mom says.

"Nothing," I say. "I was talking to myself."

I click over and check my email. I try not to be hopeful, so I open it casually, like I'm not at all excited about what might be in there. (Everyone knows that if you sneak up on news, it's more likely to be good than bad.)

My email is empty except for a cartoon from Iris of a guy on Mars holding up his iPhone and shouting, "They said there would be 5G here!" (ha-ha), a coupon from Old Navy, and a reminder that on the first day back at school we need to bring our supplies OR ELSE (it doesn't say or else *what*, exactly), and then it lists the supplies. I have no idea how a seventh-grader can need eighteen glue sticks, but there it is. I'm kind of assuming now that seventh grade isn't going to be very challenging. I hope we're allowed to have actual sharp scissors for all the cutting and gluing we'll apparently need to be doing.

There are no messages from Mars Now or from Tig. I close the computer and lay my head on it. The smooth, silver surface of the lid is hot under my cheek. The light on the side glows and subsides, glows and subsides, like the computer is breathing.

"It's alive!" I whisper. I pat it. "Good boy."

When Tig grows up, he is going to make a whole new kind of laptop computer. Instead of being a box that opens and closes and burns patterns onto your legs, it's going to be soft, like an animal or one of those microwavable bags of beans, made to nestle into our laps, not to slide off when we reach up for a glass of water. Tig was always spilling water on his laptop. Don't do that. It's a terrible thing to do.

"Not a person shape, though," he said. "That would be creepy."

"Right," I agreed. "No one wants a person on their lap."

"Exactly," said Tig, who had steadfastly refused to sit on Santa's lap every year. His parents had a whole row of photos of him with Santa on the wall in the front hallway of their house, Tig standing seriously beside Santa — never sitting on him — with his list of requests in his hand.

Tig says having a soft laptop will make us feel less alone on Mars, although social media will eventually make it so that we're actually more alone all the time, even if we never leave the Earth. He says internet relationships are easier than real ones, which may be true, but he doesn't seem to want to have an internet relationship with me now that he's gone, so I guess even an easy thing with me isn't worth the trouble.

You think you know a person and then *bam*! you don't.

I open the computer back up and drag my file labeled "photos of us" to the trash. Those pictures are all of Tig and me and the stuff we've done and built and climbed and explored and the places we've been. There are 1,008 photos. The background photo on my screen is a picture of us taken at tree-climbing camp. We went so high up that redwood, we could see the lights of LA. It was windy up there and the trees bent and waved, but the one we were on held still, like it knew we were scared, like it knew we needed it to do that. We had ropes around our waists and spikes on our toes. It was so scary and so perfect at the same time. I can practically still feel how rough the bark was and smell the soft tang of the sap. I close my eyes for a second, then I open them and change it to a photo of Mars taken on the most recent mission. It looks like there is a woman standing in the wind in a long dress. I love that photo. I put the tree-climbing shot in the trash with the 1,008 others. It feels good to do that, but I don't empty the trash bin. I can't. Not yet.

I wish I could go through my brain-memory and scrub everything Tig-related away, leaving clean spots, empty files that I can fill up with new, non-Tig things, like maybe a whole new language or the song lyrics from every song that came out in the year I was born.

Right now, I'm working on emptying my brain's memory-file of the raft we built last summer. It had a sail made from a white sheet. The raft part was made from pallets we got from the Home Depot parking lot and hammered together in the back yard. We called it the S. S. *Rafty* because neither of us is very good at coming up with names for things. We sailed the S. S. *Rafty* to Lunch Island almost every day until he left. Lunch Island is the rocky lump that rises out of the lake about two hundred feet from shore. It features some scrub brush and a glen of gnarled, dead trees that somehow are still standing. We ate peanut butter-and-cucumber sandwiches, and huge hunks of watermelon for dessert. We drank lemonade made with too many lemons and not enough sugar. Our mouths puckered and stung with every gulp, but we kept drinking. We swam races and then lay on the rocks to warm up. We read books and made plans. We agreed that the things we'd miss most when we live on Mars were lakes and rivers and the sea, not that either of us ever went to the coast.

"But after the terraforming, we'll have lakes and trees and all that," Tig had insisted. Tig was a big believer in terraforming, like we could seed the whole planet with trees and eventually they'd exhale enough oxygen that we could breathe.

But I didn't think that would happen. I know we'll live on Mars, but it will be inside biomes. Perchlorate is a real problem! Tig and I used to have big arguments about perchlorate. He was sure that perchlorate-eating bacteria would take care of it and then Mars would be as green and blue as the Earth, flourishing and safe. A small part of me doesn't want that to be true. It doesn't feel as brave. It doesn't feel as new. I could never explain that to Tig. I should have known we wouldn't stay friends forever. We had that perchlorate-issue niggling between us like a future disaster.

Anyway, hardly anyone swam in the lake anymore except for me and Tig, back then. We were braver than everyone. We wouldn't be scared off by toxic sludge! No way. Not us. We'd dive right into possible-perchlorate stew.

One day, we carved our initials into the one tree on Lunch Island with a sharpened rock. We wrote "TD & ML, Planet Earth, July 2015, forever friends." We wrote "We were here" and made an X out of pebbles to show the exact spot. We planted a signpost that said MARS: 140 MILLION MILES. (That's an average, as I'm sure you know. The distance shrinks and grows all the time because Mars's orbit is an oval. It comes closer and then moves farther away depending where it is on its path. Earth's is pretty much a circle. I wanted to write "average" beside the number, but Tig said that would be too confusing to regular people.)

I try and I try and try to erase these memories but the more I try, the more details I think of, like the bee sting I got just after we planted the sign and how I screamed. Tig made me a compress out of lake reeds to use until we could get back home. When he pressed it on my skin, he leaned his face really close to mine. I would never tell anyone this, but I think he almost kissed me and then he changed his mind. His breath was lemon-sour, but I bet mine was, too. He was so close that I could see the tiny flakes of dry skin around his nostrils. I didn't want him to do it. I held my breath. But then he didn't do it and right away, I felt sad that he didn't. Stupid, huh.

I squeeze my eyes shut tight, trying to block it all out. I wish you could stop memories. I wish you could wipe your own brain's hard drive clean.

When I open my eyes again, Mom is staring at me. "Are you OK? Do you have another headache?"

"No," I lie. "I'm fine. Well, a bit of one. Maybe."

She nods. "You've been getting lots of headaches," she says. "I have to remember to schedule you an appointment with the doctor. Note to self! Make that appointment." She taps her nose, like she's sealing that information in.

"Mom," I say. "It's just the seasons changing. You know that air pressure changes when the seasons change. Tons of people get headaches when it happens! It's normal. Also, I don't want to go to a doctor." I don't want to explain to her that the headaches are also from the work of emptying out all the Tig-memories, leaving glittering achy holes behind. No doctor would be able to figure that out. Doctors don't understand that stuff.

"Nothing from Mars Now yet?" she asks.

"Nope," I say.

"Tig?"

"Double-nope."

Then she goes, "He's probably just — "

"Mom, don't make excuses for him. DTM. Remember? Dead. To. Me. Iris says hi," I add, even though she didn't.

Mom smiles. Thinking about Iris makes everyone happy. I wonder what it would be like to be a person who has that effect on people, a person who makes everyone smile. I'll ask Iris, one day. Maybe. I just know that if I asked, she'd laugh, showing her perfect, square teeth. She'd say, "I don't do anything special, Ish." But she does. Even her voice is special.

It's not just how she looks, it's how she is: thoughtful, gentle, kind. I don't think I'm thoughtful, gentle, and kind. I want to be, but I'm not. It's too hard. Besides, sometimes I get mad. Sometimes I forget that other people, like all those girls in my class, are real people, too. They seem pretend, like extras in a movie scene, and I'm the only real one, the only one who is taking the planet seriously while they run around and throw their candy wrappers into the wind and assume someone else is going to clean up their mess. Honestly, it's crazy-making. I don't know why Iris isn't bugged by anything. She just isn't.

I close my eyes and try to imagine that I'm more like her, calm and happy. I try to picture her apartment, which is tiny, but painted all pretty colors and perfectly arranged, everything tucked away in a little space for itself. We visited her last summer. It was hot and crowded and crazy, but I loved it. I love her. I guess that's what love is, really, just wanting to be with someone. Just wanting to breathe the same air.

I do *not* have those same feelings about Elliott.

"Ugh," I say, out loud.

"What, hon?" says Mom.

"Nothing."

"Love, love, rabbit," squawks Buzz Aldrin from his cage, like he's reading my mind.

"Shut up," I tell him. "What do you know about it?"

"Dinner in five minutes," says Mom.

I get up to set the table before she asks. That's what Iris would do. I decide that from now on, I'll try to be more like Iris. What would Iris do (WWID)? I'll ask myself, and maybe my inner Irisness will sneak up on me, maybe I'll be more like her and less like Elliott. Mom says that

Elliott and I are more alike than I think, that we're both a bit "fierce."

"Fierce?" I'd repeated, when she first said it. "I'm not fierce!"

"You are the fiercest," she said. "There's nothing wrong with that! Well, maybe a little. But at least when you're older, you won't let yourself be pushed around. It will be a good thing."

"I'm not fierce," I protested.

"And prickly," she'd added. "Fierce and prickly. Just like Elliott."

I started to cry. "I'm not fierce and prickly! You make me sound terrible! Like some kind of psychotic ... hedgehog! Or something!"

She'd laughed. "Hedgehogs are cute," she'd said, coming over and giving me a hug.

I'd pushed her away, though. No one wants to be fierce and prickly!

Except maybe Elliott, and I'm not Elliott. I'm just not.

I'm going to be Iris. I'm going to be a scientist on a Mars mission, but I'm still going to be Iris. You'll see. I'll be the nicest.

If I really put my mind to it, I can do anything. I know I can. I can even be kind and happy. I think I can do that.

I stick a smile onto my face and open the laptop back up so I can see it in the camera. It looks too toothy. I dial it back a bit. I shrink my smile until it's barely there, so just a tiny sliver of my teeth show. Perfect.

"Kind and happy," I murmur to myself. "Kind and happy."

"Rabbit," says Buzz Aldrin.

"Rabbit," I agree, with the gentlest possible smile on my face. *Just* like Iris.

I feel nicer already.

5

Mom starts cutting thick slices of whole-wheat bread and laying it out on colorful plates. She adds a leaf of something on the side of each plate, a curlicue of cucumber. I love the smell of cucumber. (More TIWM: the smell of cucumber; the clatter of plates on the kitchen island; the way Mom makes everything prettier than it has to be, strictly speaking.)

"Honey, I heard on a talk show today that it actually takes years to get to Mars. Even if they do accept you, you'd just be on the spaceship for your entire life. Think of all the things you'd miss!"

"Mom," I say. "It doesn't. That's an old lie, that it would take that long. Or maybe you're thinking of Pluto? It takes forever to get to Pluto and Pluto's not even a real planet anymore, so it's not like NASA will be sending anyone there. Anyway, it only takes nine months to get to Mars. Because of orbits. I've told you this! Mars gets super close to us." I smile my nice, new, gentle smile but she doesn't notice, so I keep talking. I could talk about Mars forever. "I actually think all the time about the stuff I'll miss. I just wouldn't miss any of it *enough*. Besides, I store it all in here." I tap my head with my finger. "If I don't go, who will? Someone has to be the first. Think about it. It's basically the most important thing ever."

"Well, Ish," she says. "I guess the thing is that *I'd* miss *you*." She stirs some tuna salad in a bowl, the fork *tink-tink*ing against the metal like a tiny silver hammer against my tin skull. "I'd have you up here," she taps her own head. "But it's not the same. It's not *this*." She gestures around our kitchen, which looks like a page out of an Ikea catalogue, all pale blue and shiny and clean, like the inside of a Swedish kid's perfect dollhouse.

I roll my eyes. "Mom, don't," I say. "It won't happen for a long time. Ten years! By then you'll be glad to be rid of me! I'll be older than Iris is now!"

"But she's in New York, not outer space! Going to Mars is different. Even just the trip would destroy your brain," she says. "Your beautiful brain. I clicked a link on Facebook and I read that apparently they figure that everyone who goes will get dementia. By the time you landed — if you didn't crash — you'd all be too confused to remember why you were there. You'd probably beat each other to death with your Mars tools and things. That is, if your muscles weren't wasted away by the lack of gravity. But instead, you'll just sit there, all slumped over because your bodies won't work, wondering how you got there and how you'll get home."

Mom works in an old-folks' place called Country Acres. It's right between the regular mall and the outlet mall. It's truly awful. It's the ugliest building known to man. I'll bet the people who live there think they've died and gone straight to Hell. Old people should get to live in beautiful places! There should be some kind of prize for just living that long! Of course, when I'm old, I won't be here. I'll be in an old-folks' biome on Mars, probably shouting advice at the young people about oxygen levels and things. The biggest problem with living in biomes is the oxygen level. If it goes out of kilter, even the tiniest bit, you start to go nuts. But you don't know you're going nuts, you just really believe that suddenly everyone on your team is trying to kill you or whatnot. Then when someone tells you it's because the oxygen levels are wonky, you don't believe them, because you know for sure that they whisper about you behind your back.

The oxygen levels are perfectly fine on Earth (as far as I can tell), but I still know that people are whispering about me. It's hard not to be whispered about when you have red hair and freckles and your best friend is a boy and you want to move to Mars. It's just my lot in life. I get it. I'm fine with it. Especially now that I'm a new, more Iris-like Ish, without a boy best friend, or even a best friend at all.

"*Mom*," I say. "It won't be like that. That's to do with pressure and oxygen and not moving around enough. They understand it, so they'll fix it before we leave. They aren't going to say, 'Well, we know this trip will make you mad, but off you go, good luck!' It's NASA, not …

I don't know what. But Mom, NASA. Or even Mars Now. No one is going to do that. It would wreck their reality show, for one thing."

"Hmm," she says.

Mom is able to say more with a single "Hmm" than anyone else I know. This "Hmm" said, "Well, Ish, I think you are living in a fantasy that one day will come crashing down and break your heart."

"I don't have a heart to break," I tell her.

"What?" she says.

"Oh," I say. "It's a poem."

"Really?" she says. She gets all excited about poetry. "Did you write it?"

"*Mom*," I say, forgetting to be Iris. "No. I don't write poetry."

"How does the rest of it go?"

"I forget," I say. "Um, how was work?"

She sighs. "Pretty rough," she says.

Mom deals with bent-over, befuddled people all day long who mostly think they are just there waiting for a cab or a friend or a doctor. "Excuse me," they say. "Will my ride be here soon? I'm sure I left the oven on. I have to get home!" Then they get for-real worried about their imaginary oven in a house they haven't owned for twenty years, a house a whole different family has moved into and grown up in and moved on from. It's the saddest thing.

When I visit her at work, I can hardly stand it: Those

old people's rheumy eyes, dribbling tears down their craggy cheeks. "Are you my granddaughter?" they ask me, holding on to my arm just a bit too tight. "Why is your hair so red? Must have come from the other side of the family!" Sometimes I say yes and I let them hug me and pet my hair and I eat their dusty pocket mints and tell them that I love school, yes, and my favorite subject is science, and yes and yes and yes and I love you, too. Sometimes a whole paragraph of lies is way nicer than the one terrible truth that exists inside the word *no*.

"At least no one hit you," I say, brightly. That's the kind of positive response Iris would have.

Mom half-laughs. "Well, that's true," she says.

One day, a sweet old man with twinkly eyes named Mr. Brighton hit Mom so hard with his cane that he broke her arm. She said that she'd just told him that Bob Barker didn't work at *The Price Is Right* anymore, that Drew Carey has been hosting it for years. He couldn't believe her. "You're a liar!" he shouted. Then he came at her. Mom had a bright pink cast on for a month.

She rubs that arm now, like just thinking about her hard day makes it ache again.

Dad interrupts by stomping into the room to get a glass of water. "Stomping" makes him sound mad or something, but he isn't, it's just how he walks. He's a heavy walker, which is surprising because he's super fit and thin. He is also crazy about hydration. And I mean *crazy*. I think he may have a problem. He may be single-handedly to blame for the water shortage. Well, him and the ruined climate, obviously.

"Timing is everything," he says, for no reason, the water from his special reverse-osmosis-filtering water jug *glug-glug*ging into his ice-filled glass. I'm not sure what he is talking about, really.

"Okaaaaaay, Dad," I say. "Way to pay attention."

"What?" he says. "What?" He has this way of scratching his head and looking perplexed that makes me laugh.

"Never mind," I say, giggling.

Anyway, he's rightish about timing. But he's wrong, too. Timing is not everything. Nothing is everything. Only everything is everything! I open my mouth to say that, but he interrupts: "Anyone want some water?"

"*No*," say Mom and I at the same time.

"Overhydration is a thing, you know," Mom says. "People die."

"Pffft," he says. "We're made of water."

"Well, *you* are," Mom says, rolling her eyes at me.

I laugh again. I bet if you popped Dad with a knitting needle, he'd spray water out like a sprinkler. I'm surprised he doesn't slosh when he walks.

"You should have some water, Ish," says Dad. "No water on Mars, you know. You'll miss having water. Especially drinkable water."

"There totally *is* water on Mars," I tell him. "Don't you watch the news? But I hate drinking water," I say, which is the truth. "Plus, it will be contaminated there with perchlorate. Anyway, I won't miss it at all. Did you know that you can stay hydrated without ever having water? It's true. Besides, we'll have equipment to extract water from — "

"Red," says Elliott, who has just appeared out of nowhere. "No one is going to choose a twelve-year-old girl to go to Mars." She swings open the fridge door and shoves her head inside, emerging with a hunk of cheese sticking out of her mouth. She leaves the fridge door open and leans on the center island, chewing wetly. "You're such an idiot," she says, almost as an afterthought.

"Shut up, jerk," I say. "Settlement missions won't be going for at least — "

"You're embarrassing. No wonder you don't have any friends. This Mars thing is a joke. It's never going to happen. And even if it does, there is zero chance," she says, tilting her head closer to me, "*zero* chance that you will be on board. Which is too bad for us. Because we're stuck with you." When she speaks, her mouth opens so wide that I can see the cheese disintegrating inside and glomming itself onto every bump and space in her teeth. It's so terrible that I can't even answer her. I have to close my eyes.

"Ell," says Dad. "Please don't talk and eat at the same time. And don't bully your sister. It's good to have a goal. You could stand to have a few goals yourself."

Elliott says, "Oh, have another glass of water, Dad."

Then she laughs. When she laughs, it's like the whole room sighs with relief. Even the walls relax a bit.

Elliott and I found out two years ago that we were adopted. She is actually the only person I know who is my blood relative. I feel a bit bad, but my first thought was, "Why couldn't it have been Iris?" Elliott's first thoughts were mostly anger based. I can sort of understand why she was mad about it. Who waits until their kids are ten and twelve before dropping that bombshell on them during a spring break vacation in Disneyland? In the photos that were taken at the top of the rides (the Tower of Terror, Splash Mountain, the Matterhorn) both Elliott and I look completely blank. Not scared, not laughing, not screaming with our arms in the air like everyone else, just expressionless, like we're in shock, which I guess we were.

But I don't think it's as big of a deal as Elliott does. At least, not anymore. I feel like if I sliced my feelings about it up into a pizza, it would be equal sizes of surprised, sad, mad, and A-OK. Elliott's would be a whole anger pie. She's freshly furious about it every day. It's kind of impressive, actually. I can't stay mad about anything for that long. At least, I don't think I can. I might be mad at Tig forever, though, so maybe that's another thing we have in common. We'll see.

"Tuna salad for dinner," Mom says in her chirpy trying-to-keep-the-peace voice. "It will be ready soon."

"Well, shoot," Elliott says, all slow and loud, "I'm

gonna go to Pedro's to swim. Maybe his mom is cooking something real. His real Mom. Real cooking. Get it?"

"*Real*ly, Elliott?" Mom says. "That's enough. Nothing has changed. You're still my daughter. You're just my chosen daughter. And I love you." She blinks: *tick, tick, tick.* I can hear it from here.

Elliott has issues, in case this hasn't been clear up until this point. But she is my blood relative, so I feel like I should probably defend her. "You did say it was OK if we made playdates without asking now that we're older," I remind Mom.

"That's right, *Mom*," says Elliott. "I'm going to have a *playdate* with *Pedro*." She snort laughs. "Playdates!" she repeats, gleefully.

What would Iris do? She wouldn't cry, that's for sure, so I blink back my tears and try to go to my happy place. That is a place without Elliott. My happy place is Mars. I close my eyes and imagine my body, encased in its orange (white? green? yellow?) EVA suit, the attached boots stirring up the Mars dust. I think about how the Earth would shine in the sky like a distant star. I would watch Phobos, Mars's bigger moon, tracing its quick orbit across the sky. The thing about Phobos is that it is doomed. It's too close to the surface of Mars and it's already covered with long cracks because of the pull of the tides. One day, it's going to shatter. Then Mars is going to get a ring, like Saturn. A ring of Phobos.

"I'm going to change," Elliott announces as she

leaves the room, ignoring the tension that shimmers like pavement on a hot day.

"Jay," Mom says. "We need to do something. We need to fix this."

"Oh, for goodness' sake," says Dad. "We messed up, we did it wrong, but are we going to be punished for that forever? We shouldn't have told them at all!"

"But we had to tell them. They had to know," Mom says. "Elliott's just . . . Well, I don't know what, really."

"Mad," I say, helpfully.

"Mad," agrees Mom. "But not always. Maybe it's getting a bit less? She has a right to be upset, if you think about it."

"She's been mad for two years," I say. "It's a long time." Then I shut my mouth. Iris wouldn't have said that. "I'm sure she doesn't mean it," I add, lamely. "No one is perfect. It's fine. She'll be fine. She'll come to terms with it, like I did! I'm glad you adopted me. I like you. I love you, actually. I'm happy. Well, happyish. I am happy enough."

"Thanks, Ish," Mom says. "We love you, too."

"Me, too," says Dad. "I'm going to work out."

"It's dinner time," says Mom.

"Fine," he says. "Then I'm going to wash my hands."

Hand washing is Dad's other major interest. When he washes his hands, his phone plays a certain song for the exact length of time that he lathers, then a different song for the rinse. It's quite a procedure. If this screenwriting thing doesn't work out for him, he could be a surgeon. He's the cleanest man alive.

"I'm sorry," Mom says to me.

"Mom," I say. "Forget it. Let's talk about something else. Anything else. Or, like, not talk."

"Fair enough," she says, scooping the tuna onto the bread.

She looks so sad. I hate when she looks so sad. Why can't we just live in the moment? Right now, in this very second? I don't want to think about the past. I just want to imagine the future. I want to think about my future. The past is too painful. People should be built with erasable memories, that's a fact. We'd all be a lot happier for it.

I open the document on my laptop where I keep notes that I've written for my book. I flip through what I have so far: I've made a terrific title page, with "Misson: Mars" superimposed over my favorite photo taken on Mars's surface by the last NASA rover, with my name — Mischa Love — at the bottom in squared-off caps. It looks very serious and important and real in spite of the fact that it's hard to take someone whose last name is "Love" very seriously, even if that person is not prone to dotting her *i*'s with hearts or whatever.

I try not to make eye contact with Elliott, who is now wearing a swimsuit under a sundress, as she passes through the kitchen on her way out through the patio doors.

"Bye!" Elliott says, like nothing has happened.

She's always like that: super mad, upsetting everyone, and then completely oblivious to the havoc she has wreaked.

"Hello?" Elliott says. "Can no one hear me? I said BYE!"

"Bye," I mumble. I type a string of random letters and then delete them so that I look busy and important and not bothered by what she's done.

Mom takes a big breath, "Have fun, sweetheart."

"Shut up, shut up, shut up," Buzz Aldrin says.

"Oh, shut up yourself," says Mom. "That old bird."

"Eleanor," says Buzz Aldrin. "Pretty pretty pretty."

Elliott's real name is Eleanor, but if you dare to call her Eleanor, she will stuff you in the downstairs closet and lock the door and not let you out until your mom calls the police because you've been missing for an entire day. (This happened in May. I didn't mind, though. I like the closet. Small spaces make me feel safe.)

But still, I will not miss *Eleanor* when I go to Mars, same gene pool or not.

I have applied to be part of the Mars Now private settler program forty-seven times so far. I have forty-six emails thanking me for my interest and explaining that only a few will be chosen and I am not one of them. The emails link to a site where I can buy Mars Now merchandise. I already have pretty much one of every-thing. I don't wear any of the clothes. I just fold them up and store them in my dresser. It seems dumb to wear them here on Earth, but by the time I get to Mars, they won't fit. I can't explain why I want them anyway; I just do. They mean something. They mean everything.

I send in one more application, just for fun, even though the most recent rejection has yet to arrive. I like filling them in. I know all the answers by heart now. There are only a few questions. Not one of them is hard.

One of these times, I'll get a yes.

Maybe this time, fingers crossed.

Or maybe, eventually, I'll just be old enough to count for something, to finally be someone who matters.

6

I sleep in the hammock on the last night of school vacation. The hammock is ropy and will leave a pattern of diamond dents on my skin, but I don't care. It's technically not very comfortable but I love sleeping outside where the breeze can swing me a little bit and the night can be above me and below me, cooling my skin on all my diamond shapes. And besides, I can't be a person who cares too much about comfort. Mars is going to be uncomfortable. That's just a fact.

The night is hot and dry, which is no big surprise, because it's always hot and dry now, even when it seems like it should be cool. But it always feels like a surprise. Like, it's nighttime! Why isn't it cool yet? It feels like the coolness is being held back somehow, like all the air is yearning to let go of the heat it's holding but it can't unclench itself enough to do it. (That made sense in my head, but now I'm not so sure.)

All night long, I swing and wake up and dream more and swing more and sweat a lot. It's like sleep is right there but I can't quite get all the way into it. But I'm tired! I want to be asleep! I'm lying down with my eyes closed! The hammock moves when I shift my weight and it makes me feel strange and loose, like I could fall, like I'm already falling. But when I open my eyes, I find out that I'm not. I'm just lying here, safe as anything.

There are a million billion stars shining through the blackness and it's totally worth it to be out here even though I can't sleep. The constellations slide by above me so slowly I can barely see it happening unless I close my eyes for a bit and then open them again. I see three falling stars (which are really just meteors, but it's prettier to think of them as stars). Tonight, the moon is a crescent, and if you follow the end from the upper tip of the crescent, you can see Mars. It's blurry and so so so so so small. I can't believe I'll go there one day. I mean, I know I *will*, it's just hard to really imagine being that far away, being in a hammock on Mars (in a biome, of course), looking at a blurry Earth.

I get out of the hammock and walk around a bit. I go down to the lakeshore and stick my feet in the water. In the dark, the water is black. At least it is cool. I swish my feet around for a few minutes and then I see some bubbles rising a few feet away. Leeches scare me, even though I've never even seen one, so I jump up and get my feet on dry land. My wet feet are shiny in the moonlight. They look metallic. I look alien. This is what Martians would look like, I think. Not cute little purple guys. Just shiny, metallic people who are immune to heat or prickly grass. Or leeches, for that matter. They'd be more like machines than us.

One of the most incredible things about settling Mars is that eventually the people who go there will evolve to the conditions. Isn't that crazy to think about? They'll become different from Earth people! Better. Tougher. We'll create actual Martians in our own image, like God. If you believe that kind of thing, which I don't. I don't think. Really, it will be more like we're the cavemen and the real Martians will be our babies' babies' babies' babies. Me — Ish Love of Lake Ochoa, California — I will be the matriarch of Martians! Not that I want to have babies or things like that. I'll be pretty busy doing science experiments and making it possible for humans to stay alive.

But maybe. Who knows?

I walk along the shoreline a short distance. I'm not scared. I like being outside at night when no one else is around. I like how the air moves and I can hear the water lapping at the shore and the sound of me, breathing, my footsteps crunching a bit on the beach and the trees rustling. I throw a rock into the water and it makes a really satisfying *bloooop* sound, so I throw another and another until my arm starts to ache.

Then I go back home and try to get comfortable in the hammock. I make myself close my eyes and I count slowly to ten and then back from ten and then up to ten again and then back. That was Tig's trick. He said it got distracting when you went above ten, and he's right. I can't get much further than fifteen without my mind wandering, but maybe a wandering mind is the point.

When I finally properly dream, I'm on Mars and have stepped out of the airlock without my protective suit. The perchlorate! I'm inhaling it! The air is just like real air, but I know it isn't. I know — in my dream — that I'm doomed and I start to cry, but not sobbing-crying, just tears leaking down my cheeks. "But I'm not finished!" I keep saying. Then I get really dizzy. My eyes keep shutting. It's too bright, somehow, and I can't see properly. I keep trying to look at things, but they stay out of focus. Even though I blink hard, the dusty ground and the orange sky just get blurrier and blurrier and grayer and lighter and I'm fading and I'm fading and I'm fading and I can't even scream. I feel so sad. I'm not done! I'm dying, but I'm not ready! But I know there's no one who can help me. I can't see anyone. No one is out here but me. I'm alone. In the dream, everything fades and fades until it's all the palest pinkish white and my chest hurts from trying to breathe in the fog and then I die. I think I actually die. You aren't supposed to die in dreams, but I do. I did.

I wake up sad and shivering hard, even though it isn't even a bit cold. A moth lands on my arm. I feel each foot like a tiny little eyelash, resting on my bare skin. Usually I have my notebook with me to sketch things like this, so I can remember them, but I must have left it on my desk. When I'm on Mars, noticing things and sketching them will be super important for cataloguing. Cameras might not work. It's not like you can go down to Best Buy and get a new one if yours breaks. It's going to be old-fashioned: drawing, cataloging. I mean, obviously we'll have cameras, too, but I've been practicing my sketching just in case. Plus, I like doing it.

Anyway, there won't be any moths.

I blink hard to clear my eyes, which are still sleep-blurry. Sometimes it takes me a long time in the morning to get them to focus properly. When the moth takes off, I can see that the undersides of his wings are really bright blue. It's so cool. "Come back!" I tell him, but he ignores me. Typical. Insects never listen.

The sun is coming up over the hills in the distance, hot and angry-looking, the orange and pink spreading low and thin into the smoggy air. The sunrise leaks into the haze and pinks it up. On Mars, the sky is pinkish all the time, as far as we know. No one knows how accurate the color portrayal is on the footage the missions have brought back. I don't mind. I like pink. I mean, not on me, but it's a fine color for a sky.

The air smells different already somehow, like all the antiseptic cleaner and floor wax they use in the school has permeated everything, even the smog, and traveled all the way here. Gross. (TIWNM: the smell of the inside of the school; school, in general; being nervous about school; doing and saying all the wrong things.)

I breathe through my mouth and try not to think about today. If I were on Mars, what would I be doing? Getting up to tend crops, I'll bet. Basically, the first settlers will be glorified (but very brave!) farmers. In the corner of the yard here, I have a greenhouse that I got for my last birthday. I've covered the ground with dirt, like the guy does in my favorite Mars book, and planted it all with tomatoes (gross) and potatoes (even grosser) and other vegetables like kohlrabi (ugh) and Brussels sprouts (worse). I'm not actually a fan of vegetables, as it turns out.I make myself eat them, for practice for the future, when I'll have to eat to survive for real.

I want to lie here all day and watch the fierce sun travel across the whole smoky blue bowl of the sky, and maybe water my plants and see if any are ready to harvest. But I can't. Not today.

"Save meeeeeee," I say to the sun, which doesn't answer.

One day, the sun will implode. It's just a star, one of a billion stars. One day, our sun will turn into elements. Of course, by then, we'd better have figured out a way to get to a different galaxy, because when the sun goes out, it's lights out — permanently — for all of us. (I don't mean to be such a downer, but it's true.)

"Sorry," I say out loud to the sun. "Keep burning, OK?"

Iris would never be so pessimistic. But maybe I can't be Iris. Someone has to be me! It might as well be me.

I sigh. It's hard to figure all this stuff out: who to be, how to be, what to be. It was easier when Tig was here. When Tig was here, I wasn't just me. I was us. It's easier to be an us than a me.

Iris has always had a million friends. Iris never had this problem.

If I stay outside for much longer, I'll broil like a slice of bacon on the fryer. "Get up, Love," I tell myself, sternly.

In books and movies about Mars settlements, everyone uses their last names. I don't know why. Maybe first names are an Earth thing, better left behind, with all your old memories and photos and books. I don't know if I really want to be called Love, but I guess there are worse things. (Like Red, for example. You wouldn't call someone with regular brown hair "Regular Brown," would you? I think not.)

I try to roll over so I can stand up, and somehow instead of letting me go, the hammock hangs on, wobbling, then tips. For a second, I'm tumbling. Then I land hard on the dry, dead grass, the air whooping out of me.

I try not to throw up. I lie back and watch the bright white stars drift around in my field of vision. Those are inner stars, not real ones. I wait for them to twinkle out and then I inhale, slow and deep. It takes a second to get my air back in properly, my lungs filling up like pink balloons, the sky tilting strangely above me.

"I'm a machine," I tell the tilted sky.

The sky hangs there, ignoring me.

My stomach makes that low, curdling sound it makes when it's empty. I make myself get up. I'm wobbly but OK. I go to the front door and push it, but it's locked, which is terrible news because I have to pee. I can always climb the tree and go in my window, but I can't climb properly if I have to clamp my legs together to stop myself from wetting my pants. I have to go so bad, my feet itch. Astronauts wear diapers. True story. What did you think? That there were bathrooms in space? There's nothing like that on Mars, either. Besides, pee needs to be recycled so you can drink it. Think about it.

The houses across the road are still. Probably everyone is asleep and not looking out their front windows to see what I'm up to over here. I whip my pj pants down and pee in the shrubs, careful not to get any on my feet. The plants need the water and I'm not squeamish about bodily functions, at least I'm trying not to be. To be honest, the idea of drinking my own recycled sweat and/or pee (or someone else's) is pretty unappealing. Actually, it makes me puke a bit into my own mouth. But I will be able to do it when I have to! I hope. There are probably a lot of gross things that you have to get used to pretty quickly when you're living on a whole new planet. I'm sure drinking pee won't even be the worst of it.

I walk away from the puddle and climb the tree, which has big broad leaves that are turning brown around the edges. It's dying, much like everything else. The day is already hot! I'm already sweating! Poor tree. It can't go inside where there is air-conditioning to escape all this. I pull myself up from branch to branch. The tree is pretty easy to climb, with its thick, wide boughs. The bark feels cool under my hands even though the air is stupidly hot. I love this tree. I will for sure miss this tree. But come on. I mean, I won't still be climbing it when I'm twenty-two! (At this rate, it will be dead long before I go, anyway.)

"It will probably rain soon," I tell the tree. I pat it reassuringly.

The sky is cloudless. What if it never rains again? Even the tree knows I'm lying.

Iris never lies.

"That was a lie," I say to the tree. "I'm sorry, you're going to die." That doesn't feel any better, frankly. It might have been kinder to lie. But doesn't the tree have a right to know?

The window to my bedroom is luckily pretty easy to open. I don't look down as I push myself up onto the sill and tumble over, onto my carpeted floor. It's not even seven in the morning and already my head hurts more than it should. What Mom doesn't know is that my head almost always aches, it's just a matter of more or less. I can't tell her. I just can't.

If I tell her, it will make it real. It will become a capital-T Thing. "Ish's headaches" will be a problem that everyone is trying to solve. Elliott's job in this family is to be the problem-to-solve! My job is to be the smart one. Iris's job is to be perfect. I feel like we've got that all figured out and adding a problem to the mix would wreck the balance. Besides, I have enough problems right now (see: school); adding to that is out of the question.

There was a time when I didn't have headaches and there will be a time when I don't have them again, this is the in-between part when I do. I feel like we just need rain. Real rain. Hard rain. Pouring, soaking, splattering rain. And even though it doesn't make any sense, I know my head will stop hurting if it rains. Everything will be fixed if it rains.

If.

I lie on the carpet for a few extra seconds. It smells like nylon and rubber. My bedroom is clean and perfect and totally organized. I don't have anything that I don't absolutely need, except for the pictures. Everything lines up in straight lines. The bed is made so tight, you could bounce a coin on it. All my clothes are put away. I don't keep anything for sentimental reasons. There's no room for sentimental stuff on a spaceship. I've figured out how to keep what matters inside my head. That way, I don't need anything. Or anyone.

The only thing that makes my room different from any other astronaut's quarters is that I made frames that look like window frames and put big photos of Mars's surface inside them and white curtains around them. If you didn't know better, you'd think you were looking out windows at the real thing. I'm not dumb, I know that on Mars there won't be curtains, but they make the windows look more like windows. Things like fabric will be a luxury for at least a generation. I wonder if we'll grow cotton. I wonder if someone will weave it or spin it or whatever. Or if we'll actually just keep waiting for shipments from the Earth, bringing more and more of what we wanted to leave behind from Amazon.com. Maybe Amazon will get Mars drones so it can bring us new socks and the latest season of whatever dumb show is popular and cinnamon gummy bears. It probably won't be any different from Earth, eventually. Humans are like that. We can't stop accumulating stuff. That's why we've basically wrecked the whole planet. It's why we need a new one in the first place.

I get up and start opening drawers to find what I need, then I pull on my clothes (white T-shirt/short sleeved, new jeans that go in at the bottom with little zippers, white socks, black Converse high-tops). I go into the bathroom to wash my face and brush my teeth. That's when I notice it. DOOM. I almost scream out loud, but I stop myself just in time.

All in a row on my left cheek, three mosquito bites. They are huge and red and look like boils. "Seriously," I say to my cheek. "Today of all days." I lean my forehead against the mirror and close my eyes and pretend I look like someone else, like Bea or Zoe, with their streaky blond hair, or even Ana Sofia with her curly black hair that looks as soft as feathers. Then I remember it doesn't matter. Who cares? I'd rather be smart than pretty! I'm not the pretty one, so I don't have to worry about being pretty. That's the truth. Besides I'm going to Mars! Pretty only lasts for so long. Next thing you know, you're an old person.

Life is short, that's all I mean.

I glare at my cheek. I put "mosquitoes" into my brain-room of TIWNM. Let them buzz around in there with Elliott for a while. (And wasps. And fast food. And shopping malls. And plastic water bottles. And school.) If only I could put the entire school away in that room, lock the door, and throw away the key. If only I had that kind of magic.

"I'd do anything to not have to go to school. Anything," I say out loud. I don't know who I'm talking to. I don't know anyone who has the power to make that kind of deal.

The room stays silent. Of course. I wasn't even expecting anyone to answer. Not really. Not this time.

I was just hoping. Sometimes hope is all you've got to hang on to, like the one thing that's tethering you to the ship while all of the Universe threatens to pull you away from the tin can spaceship that's keeping you safe and alive.

7

I'm halfway down the stairs when Elliott's door flings open and she comes tearing out. Something you might not guess about Elliott is that she *loves* school. (I know, I don't get it either.) Elliott is really really really good at sports. School is her thing because there are sports there. Her main sport is wrestling. Don't ask.

"Gooooooood morning, little red freakazoid!" she shouts, shoving me down the last five steps.

I land hard on my feet in a way that I can feel all the way up the back of my legs. My head jangles inside like a bell with a broken clapper, a muted hammering, echoing afterward with a kind of buzz.

"Jerk," I mumble.

She ignores me and pours herself a bowl of cereal and empties all the milk into it, slopping rice puffs onto the counter in little krispie-mounds. I pour my own bowlful and start eating it, but it is so dry that I choke. I bite into an apple instead. Mealy. I sigh dramatically.

Elliott grins. "Cheer up," she says. "Maybe there will be some new weirdo kid for you to befriend."

I glare at her. "You should talk," I say, which doesn't

make sense because Elliott has plenty of friends. Wrestling friends and basketball friends and volleyball friends and track friends. The thing with sports is that they come with a built-in support system. Not so with science. Not in Lake Ochoa, anyway. Maybe there is somewhere in America where science is the cool thing and there are clubs and parties and whatnot, but that place is not here.

"Shut up," squawks Buzz Aldrin.

"You shut up," I tell him.

I pour a glass of water and make myself drink it. Yuck. I have no idea why Dad loves it so much. It tastes slightly like chemicals (perchlorate?) and sweat.

"You can do this. You have to do this. It will be fine. You're invisible. You're a machine. You're OK," I murmur to myself. I will be my own inner-Iris! "You've got this!" I experimentally bite into an apple from the other side of the bowl. It's OK. It's better than the first one. I hope we can grow apples on Mars. Even when they are mealy, they still leave a good taste behind.

"I'm invisible," mimics Elliott. "You wish. Hey, what would you do if you were invisible? I'd just go around and take photos of everyone picking their noses. Everyone does it, but they all pretend it's gross. Then I'd glue them up in the hall at school so that they couldn't be ripped down."

"Huh," I say. I snicker. She's probably right.

"You'd probably do something boring though, right? Like . . . go spy on Tig?"

I flinch. I mean, yes, I probably would. "No," I go. "He's dead to me." I spit the last bite of apple into the trash. For some reason, I suddenly can't swallow it.

"Don't freak out," she says, which is pretty much as kind as Elliott gets. "Just hope you don't get Wall. He'll totally pick on you. He doesn't like smart kids. He likes sports."

"I like sports," I lie. "I like running."

"True," Elliott says. She smiles at me. When she smiles, she's so pretty, it's ridiculous. Sometimes I forget that she's pretty, because she's so mean. "You've got mosquito bites on your face," she observes.

"I *know*," I snap. "Leave me alone, OK?"

She raises her hands in mock fear. "OK! *Sorrrrrry*." She puts her cereal bowl in the sink. "DAD!" she shouts. "WE'RE GOING TO BE LATE!"

Elliott and I used to be sort-of-friends. It's like when Dad told us about the adoption, she just got so mad at me that she forgot that part. We used to play games together all the time. Old-timey board games, like Monopoly and Life. When we went camping, we'd always share a tent and we'd take a whole pile of those dumb games and play for hours, the sunlight coming through the nylon walls tinting everything blue. It was the greatest. Then, one time when I won, she got really mad and stuffed my game piece up my nose. (I was the car. My nose was never quite the same after that. I swear my right nostril is still bigger than my left.) She's always been super competitive. After that, Mom and Dad let us each have our own tent and that big old blue tent got thrown away. We never slept in the same one again. At first, because it was fun, but then because she couldn't stand me. I think that's when I started to like being by myself best of all, those camping trips where I could just crawl into my tent and get away from everyone.

Anyway, like they say, you can pick your friends but not your family. Except in the case of our family, when Mom and Dad *did* pick us. But did they really? It's not like they had a rack of babies to choose from. They just came up on a list and bam, they got babies. They got us, whether we were their choice or not. Sometimes I wonder if we were a package deal, and they picked Elliott because she was so cute, only to find out they had to take the red-headed baby, too, so they got stuck with me. Maybe I've been a tiny bit mad at Elliott ever since then, for being cuter, for being the one that brought me along for the ride.

Maybe.

Dad comes into the room, jangling his car keys. "Well," he says. "Ready for lift-off?"

"Past ready," says Elliott. "Let's just go! I don't want to be late."

"OK, OK," says Dad. "Move out, troops."

I grab my lunch out of the fridge.

"Hurry up," groans Elliott. "Seriously."

"I'm coming," I say.

"No fighting," says Dad, automatically.

"Yes, sir," we say, together.

Elliott catches my eye for a half-second and winks, but then she's gone, out the door, loping across the dead grass to the car. That half-second is about as close as she comes these days to being a sister. I guess I'll take it.

"Hey," Dad says, looking at me in the mirror as I throw my heavy backpack into the backseat and climb in after it. "What do you get when you cross a cow with an octopus?"

"Not in the mood, Dad," I say. The air in the car is as hot and impossible to breathe as Jell-O. "Maybe you'd just be arrested?" (It's illegal to crossbreed animal species. True fact.)

"You're so literal," he says, but he's grinning. "Nope, the answer is a cow that can milk itself."

"Ha ha," I say, flatly. "Oh em gee, hilarious."

"Tough crowd," says Dad.

Elliott has her headphones on and is banging on the dashboard like it's a bongo drum. Each bang goes into my head and shivers down my neck. I swallow to keep from feeling sick. My mouth tastes like apple. I can't remember if I brushed my teeth.

"Excited about school?" Dad asks. "New school year, probably some new kids, so new friends, right?"

"Dad," I say. "Seriously? No."

"Oh," he says. "OK. Want me to tell you more jokes to cheer you up?"

I look out the window, at Tig's old house as we go by. Then the Bishops'. And the Navarros'. Someone new has moved into the Munros'. For a second I imagine that Dad is right, that a new kid means that I could have a new friend, then I erase that thought immediately. I don't need a new friend. I need my old friend back. There is a new shed in the front yard. It has a huge sign on the front of it, bright orange, that says, "TRESPASSERS ARE NOT ALOUD." I grin. That sign will get a visit from me and my red pen later.

"Ish?" says Dad.

"Um, no," I say. "Thanks anyway."

I close my eyes and I can see Tig's house imprinted there, yellow and cracked, a wasps' nest hanging over the front door.

Last Tuesday, I snuck inside that house. The back door was unlocked. I didn't really mean to go in, but when the handle turned and the door swung open, I couldn't help it. I don't know why I did it, why I even tried. Going in felt wrong, but not wrong enough to stop me. It's like I thought that if I kept looking, I might find Tig in there.

The house looked weird and sad without any furniture in it, without any stuff on the walls, like how clothes look when they are on hangers, without anyone in them to fill them out. There were dents in the carpet where everything used to be: the dining room table and chairs; the sofa and coffee table; the ugly orange lamp that got so hot that I burned my hair on it when I stood up too fast one time after falling asleep watching *Star Wars*; and the aquarium table where the bright yellow and blue tangs swam around in circles, bumping against the glass like they thought they could swim right through and out into the room, out the front door, and down the road to the lake. They were salt-water fish. The lake would have killed them! But, of course, they didn't know that. Fish aren't very self-aware, even ones with smart-sounding names like "surgeonfish." It's not like they went to medical school. Or any type of school, except a school of fish. (Ba dum cha!)

I walked around every room and ran my hand over the walls, feeling all the bumps and dents and bubbles under the stripy wallpaper. There were clean marks where the Santa pictures used to hang, a row of rectangles of brighter yellow than the rest. I climbed up the thickly carpeted stairs to Tig's old room and lay on the spot where the bed used to be. I looked up at Tig's old ceiling, like he must have done a million times. There were marks where he'd pinned the satellite maps of Mars that we printed off the internet at the public library. The room smelled a bit like socks. I wonder if he stuck those maps up in his new room in Portland. I bet he didn't. I bet that he just threw them away, like everything else that used to matter to him. I tried to list all the major craters on Mars: Hellas Planitia, Utopia Planitia, the Borealis Basin.

Then I noticed that there were little brown pellets all over the carpet. Gross. Rats.

I got up pretty quick, so quick that I got dizzy. (Rats are another thing I definitely won't miss on Mars. I hope that none stow away with the supplies, somehow arriving there first and taking over the planet. I bet rats would adapt. Animals do that. You can drop a nuclear bomb and the animals will just evolve to survive in the post-Apocalyptic wasteland. Look at Chernobyl! There are all kinds of weird animals living there now, with two stomachs or weird body temperatures. Humans don't adapt. We just get cancer and die and that's the end of it, for us. Depressing if you think about it, so I don't recommend it.)

"OK," Dad says, suddenly, startling me out of my daydream. "Fine. Be that way. I had a great riddle about a pirate and a cow, though . . ."

"I'm not being any way," I say. "I was just thinking."

"Thinking is good," he says. "Fair enough."

"YEAH!" shouts Elliott. Her eyes are closed and she's still hammering on the dashboard.

I wonder what it's like to be her. She does so much to hide what she looks like so people won't look at her because she's pretty, but then she does all this other stuff that kind of demands an audience. I bet she doesn't even know why she does that. I don't know why I do the stuff that I do. But it's easy to see in other people. I sometimes think there are two layers of all of us: who we are and what we look like. They are completely different parts and one doesn't necessarily know what the other is doing.

We drive the rest of the way without talking. When we arrive, I lean over the seat and give Dad a quick kiss. Poor Dad. He tries so hard. He's just always slightly out of step. He smells so Dad-like, like toothpaste and soap and bleach, that I feel like I might cry.

"Want me to come in with you?" he asks me.

"No way," I tell him.

I brace myself and pull my pack onto my shoulders. It turns out that all those glue sticks are quite heavy. It's a good thing I've been working out. "I'm a machine," I whisper, and in I go, swallowed into the belly of Theodore Roosevelt Middle School, which looks exactly like you'd imagine: like every school, ever. Ancient linoleum floors, worn down to gray in the middle of the halls. Rows of light blue and yellow lockers. Safety posters, and windows that are too high to escape through. Fire alarm pulls with big signs above them saying PULL IN CASE OF FIRE ONLY. Red EXIT signs. "I wish I could," I tell the signs. "Exiting is my favorite."

It's the smell that I hate the most: the floor wax and all the other people and boy-sweat and papery mold and who knows what. My headache is so bad, it feels like someone is cupping my brain with their hand and then squeezing really hard, like one of those stress balls that Dad keeps on his desk. I tug at my long ponytail, which relieves the pressure just a tiny bit. Then I find my name on the posted list. LOVE, MISCHA. 114. I make my way down the hallway, following the signs to the classroom: Mr. Wall's Grade 7A. All along the way, those high windows show the sky outside and the sun filters in and lights up the dust. I kind of think we're all like that dust, actually. Sometimes, when the sun shines on us, just for a second, we're beautiful.

Then someone pushes me from behind.

"Move it, nerd," a voice says.

I brace myself against a locker and wait for them to go by.

"Happy first day of school, Ish," I say to myself, I say to no one, I say to the shining dust in the air.

"Loser," someone says.

And that's how seventh grade begins.

8

M r. Wall is a tall, skinny man with a moustache that has grown around his mouth and down onto the two sides of his chin, like a horseshoe with all the luck running out. If he would tip his head up, we could see if it met in the middle. That would make it less of a moustache and more of the letter *O*, which totally fits him, because he also has arched, high-up eyebrows that make him look perpetually surprised. He's awfully old, at least fifty, and the shoulders of his black golf shirt are sprinkled with white flakes.

"Name?" he barks at me.

"Ish," I say. "I mean, Mischa."

"Mischa," he says. "And you prefer to be called Ish?" In his mouth, the name Ish sounds terrible: all spitty and wet.

I can feel the blush blooming on my chest and crawling up my neck, where it settles on my face like a hot, clammy washcloth. "Mischa is good," I tell him.

"Ish," someone whispers in the back row and then, "Ish, Ish, Ish, Ish, Ish" spreads across the whole room like running footsteps on thick carpet. IshIshIsh. I've known most of these people forever. They've called me Ish since I was five! Why does it sound so dumb now? I want to stick my tongue out at all of them, but I bite it instead.

In Tibet, sticking your tongue out at someone is like saying hello. But this isn't Tibet. And, anyway, I don't want to say hello. What I want to say is a swear with four letters, but I won't. It wouldn't improve the start of this year to be in the principal's office, already trying to explain myself. Anyway, I don't think I could do that if I tried.

"Fish," someone says, louder than the rest, and they all burst out laughing. Everyone. Tig wouldn't have laughed. They wouldn't have laughed either, if he was here. Not really. I mean, I wouldn't have cared if they had. The difference is that I didn't need them then. Now, I guess I do.

Sweat prickles on my neck. The boy who shouted "Fish!" won't make eye contact with me, even though I try to stare him down. He's new. He has curly hair and too much of it. It's brown and so thick and tall that it looks like a wig or a joke. He gazes at the floor, a little grin on his face. I don't care who he is or where he came from, I already hate him. I hate everyone. Even Mr. Wall. And the cement blocks that make up the walls of the classroom. And especially the way the window shades block the light. The dust is probably still here, I just can't see it without the sun.

"I'm a machine," I remind myself. "Just a machine." But I can't make myself believe it.

I sit down behind Kaitlyn Brenner because it's the only empty seat except the one beside Fish-boy. Kaitlyn laughs like a donkey, *hee-haw, hee-haw,* but somehow still manages to be one of the most popular people in our grade. Her hair is done in rows and rows and rows of tiny braids, each one with a different-colored elastic at the end, like the ones in those rubber band bracelet kits, which I know she has because she's wearing about twenty bracelets on each arm. It must have taken a billion hours to braid all that hair and make all those bracelets.

"I like your hair," I lie.

"Oh," Kaitlyn says. "Thaaaaa-aa-anks." I don't know how she can even manage to make that into so many syllables.

"Yeah," I say, trying to mimic her tone. "You're welcoooo-oome." If I blend in more, they'll leave me alone. The trouble is that when I stretch words, I sound like a humpback whale, singing.

She squints, like she's not sure whether I'm insulting her or not. "Your hair is, um, brushed nice, too," she says, charitably. Kaitlyn is OK. I don't know why I feel mad at her. I guess because she's not Tig.

I laugh to fill the silence, even though nothing is funny, and she laughs, too. *Hee-haw, hee-haw.* I feel exhausted. Exhilarated, even! Contact made! Well done, Love. I would high-five myself if I could. I give myself permission to stop trying for the rest of the day or perhaps forever. (TIWNM: trying to figure out the right things to say all the time; awkward giggling fits; classrooms.)

Mr. Wall starts telling a story about how he was riding his motorcycle through the Grand Canyon in the summer and he hit a coyote that was crossing the road, wiping out his bike. He rolls up his pants and shows us the road rash. I try to force myself to look. One more thing Tig and I have in common is fainting when we see blood. "You can all come and take a closer look," Mr. Wall tells us. No one moves. "OK, then," he says cheerfully. This is the happiest he's been since I walked through the door. He's practically grinning. "Now, did everyone bring all their supplies? Let's put them all away, starting with green notebooks. *Green* notebooks, everyone."

No one asks about the coyote. Did it die? Does anyone care? I do. But it's not like I'm going to put up my hand. No way.

It's only 9:42 a.m. and already the day feels like it's taken forever. On Mars, days are 37 minutes and 22 seconds longer than on Earth. If we ever get to the point in the settlement where we have schools, I'm going to propose that those 37 minutes and 22 seconds are not spent in the classroom. This is not a good use of time! I want to scream. This is not the point of anything! It seems impossible to believe that road-rashed Mr. Wall will have anything useful to teach me that will help me survive on Mars. There should be special schools for kids who are earmarked for Mars missions. I should be learning about how to tell where I am by the stars. Or how to terraform a planet. Or how to create an atmosphere where none currently exists.

I start doodling a biome on my new agenda. I shade in all the hexagons on the glass dome faintly with pencil. I draw leaves of plants, growing up toward the sun. I sketch a Martian settler in a protective spacesuit, stepping out of the biome, onto the dusty wasteland. When I see Fish-boy staring openly at my paper, his dumb mouth hanging open, I curve my body around so he can't see it. I try not to cry even though I suddenly really really feel like crying. Crying is stupid. There won't be any crying on Mars. (I hope.)

"I am a machine," I write in perfect cursive in the blank that says Date, at the top of the page. Beside *Name*, I write "Tig," then I cross it out, then I scribble over it, and pretty soon there is just a block of black where my name should be.

By lunchtime, my headache is as big as Deimos (which is Mars's other moon, not the doomed one), and just as lumpy. I walk carefully, trying not to jostle it. We have to go outside to eat today. Mr. Wall announces this like it's a treat. The cafeteria is being painted! You get to eat outside! Does he not know there's a heat wave? Everyone groans.

The air outside is prickly and tight, like it is before a thunderstorm, but the sky is still blue and hazy, like always. The wind is barely stirring up the dust. It's just stupidly hot. There's no way to describe it beyond that. Stupid. Hot. The kind of hot where you can't think about anything else except how hot it is. The heat takes over your brain. It takes over everything. Basically it's what I imagine Hell to be like, if it exists, which isn't likely. Maybe I'm dead. Maybe this *is* Hell. Do dead people know that they are dead? If you think about it, and if you think that death is just a stopping of everything, your own infinity is the period of time of your life. Because you can't know that it's stopped, it never stops, but your own infinity is held inside your life-span, like a snail in a shell. You become your own "forever," stuck in the loop of youness. Think about it.

I pinch myself to make sure I'm not dead. I'm definitely alive, because it hurts. I sigh.

I wonder if Tig is at school or if he is being home-schooled. His mom was always talking about homeschooling, but Tig would never do it. He wouldn't have been away from me. Is he in a regular school now, like this one (but less hot)? Or is he at one of those shirt-and-tie schools? Or at home, at his regular kitchen table, his mom's long hair swooping down over the place where he's writing an essay about ancient Egypt or building a volcano out of cardboard and baking soda?

Maybe she'll make him write me a letter. Maybe she'll ask him about me and he won't be able to answer because he hasn't emailed me even once so I haven't emailed him either. Maybe he'll have to do it, when she asks, to see how I am. Maybe then he'll tell me why he didn't say good-bye. Why everything stopped.

Maybe.

I sniff. I can't start crying out here! That would be social suicide. I look around frantically for a place to be alone, so I can hide my pink, about-to-tear-up eyes.

The kids cluster around the edges of the brick buildings, pressing themselves into the shade. I go over to the one, single tree on the far side of the playground, crossing the tarmac, which burns my feet through my shoes. It's worth it just to put some distance between me and everyone else. I lean against the tree and try to look busy in my own thoughts. The tree is sticky with sap. I try to look like I don't care that I have no one to eat with. I try to look happy. Luckily, I'm not terrible at acting. I'm actually pretty good at it. Last spring, Tig's parents and my parents got together and decided that instead of just hanging out all the time, Tig and I had to choose some kind of extracurricular activity. Apart from sports, there was not a lot to choose from, so we chose acting. It was pretty silly. We made fake commercials. We laughed a lot. Most of it was laughing, to be honest. It was always hard not to laugh, even when a camera was filming all of it. But it was fun.

It was the best kind of fun because you got to be someone else, just for a few minutes at a time. You got to have a break from being yourself. I didn't have to be the smart one. I could be the airhead or the sports maniac or the mad one or whatever I wanted. It was like I folded my real self up and put myself in a drawer, just for a bit.

Tig didn't really get that, but he was from a normal family and wasn't adopted and was actually pretty good-looking and might have been good at sports if he wanted to do them, which he didn't. I bet if he hadn't had me, he would have had tons of friends. Normal friends. He was pretty OK in his own skin. I think that was my favorite thing about Tig. Now, of course, nothing is my favorite thing about Tig because he's dead to me, so honestly, I have no idea why I'm thinking about him. Although I guess even after someone dies, you can still think about the good parts about them being alive. You can still miss them.

When you know someone really well, you stop seeing what they actually look like. I think that's why Tig was my friend. If he met me now, he probably wouldn't be. Well, obviously he's chosen to stop anyway. But still, that new kid is right: I look like a fish. A goldfish. Bright orangish-red and nothing like all the other fish, all those rainbow trout glittering like silver-pink prisms in the sunlight. The lake doesn't have trout in it anymore, but it used to. I remember catching them with Elliott when we were little. I try to remember if that was fun or if she just shoved me into the water and ran away laughing, but I really can't remember.

Weird. It was definitely Before the Bad News, so she was probably normal then. She used to be. Hard to believe, I know.

Being upright is making my headache worse, so I unstick myself from the tree and lie down on my back and close my eyes, my hair fanned out in the dust. I take the ponytail out altogether. It doesn't help. I'll swim in the lake later and rinse the dust away.

I don't really mean to fall asleep, but I guess that I do, because I'm dreaming that I'm on Mars. I'm on Mars and I'm working in a biome garden in a geodesic dome and the sunlight is filtering through a pink, dusty-looking sky through the glass. I can practically feel the humidity, taste the dusty dirt-flavored air. Through the window, instead of just red dirt, I see patches of green. Things are growing out there, which is impossible but must be true because I can see it. Tig's dream has come true! Well, inside my dream.

In the dream, I'm squishing seeds down into the earth. Everything is tinged red or more like rusty orange. (The reason why Mars looks red is because it is, effectively, covered with rust. All that dirt is oxidized, which is the same thing that happens to iron when it rusts. Look it up! It's true.) I feel totally, weirdly peaceful and at home, like when we've been camping or on a trip and we come back to the house and I see my bed, and it kind of rings inside me like "Oh, finally! Home!" It's like that, times a million. I sink my fingers into the ground, put in seed after seed. I'm super excited, but I'm trying to act natural because I'm dreaming that I know it's a dream but it's not a dream. None of that makes sense, but that's OK. That's what dreams are like.

I sit back on my heels and look outside. I press my hand against a pane of the dome Plexiglas. It's cold. Solid. I look up and a big butterfly flies by me, circles, lands on my arm and takes a few steps, *plink, plink, plink* with its sticky feet. It reminds me of something. I say, "Oh!"

I lift it close to my face. On its wings, there is a perfect pattern. It looks like stained glass in a church window. I reach into a pocket on my shirt and take out a notebook and a pencil. The pencil is silver. I draw the butterfly. Of course, in the dream, I'm excellent at drawing. That's how I'm reminded that it's just a dream. At the top of the page, I write "Dream Butterfly." Just as I finish, it takes off. It's got iridescent wings, aqua blue and shimmering, like the moth this morning, which I've suddenly just remembered (but am trying not to, because it's pulling me awake, dragging me out of this amazing dream).

"It's fine," I say out loud, in the dream. "I'm on Mars. There's a butterfly. I want to stay."

The butterfly comes back into focus. I exhale. He doesn't hide his colors; they are all over him. He's huge. When the sun glints off his wings, they look purple and pink. They look every color, like a rainbow trout in the sun's beams. I get up and start to follow him. He flies crookedly, landing here and there.

I'm right back in it again, deep in the dream. So of course, I make a dumb mistake. I guess if you didn't make dumb mistakes in dreams, they'd be boring. What I do is that I forget that I'm on Mars and have to wear a suit to go outside and I follow the butterfly out an open door. (Of course, if the door were really open, I'd already have been dead! The atmosphere on Mars can't support humans. It's pretty much all carbon dioxide. Anyway, it's a dream, so whatever happens happens and it's too late, in the dream, to go back.) So I take about fifty steps outside, following the butterfly, when my eyes start to get blurry and I realize that I've died. I'm dead. In the dream, I die. You aren't supposed to be able to die in dreams, you're supposed to wake up right before you do, and this is the second time I have today!

In the dream, I'm crying because I'm dead and I'm on Mars, I made it to Mars and I did something dumb and I died, once again before I was finished, before I had done what I meant to do.

9

I wake up when the bell sounds to end lunch, and my eyes are wet from crying. I'm pretty much going to have to stop sleeping forever if every time I do, I die and cry.

"Die-and-cry," I say out loud. Tig would get that. I miss him so hard that my stomach clenches.

I wipe my eyes with my hands. My hands are brown with dust, so that probably just makes matters worse. Great. Terrific. I stand up to head back into the building, but just as I do, there's this incredible crackling sound.

I can't even describe how enormous it is, but no one else seems to notice.

CRACKLE, CRACKLE.

It's crazy! It's so loud! Like the whole world is made of thin glass and it's breaking all at once.

Then I realize that the sound isn't a sound. Not one you can hear. It's inside me. It's a crackling *inside* me. It's an inside sound that's so loud and intense, it basically fills me up. It takes over.

I open my mouth to call for help, but I can't. My tongue is stuck. My word is stuck. I can't remember how to push the word out of my throat. Is that where words come from? The word won't come out of me. It won't form properly in my mouth. My tongue is pinned down by something sharp. I'm standing now, under the tree, with my arms outstretched and my mouth open, waiting for the "Help!" to come.

Then the crackle surges and wallops me in the back of the head and I feel my skull exploding and I'm on my knees and now I am dead, I'm dead, I'm dying! I can't believe this, I can't believe this is happening. And I'm buckling forward in slow motion and I'm thinking well, this is still the dream, the third time I've died in a dream today, wow, that's weird, it's really a lot of times to die in dreams and where is the butterfly? I'm falling forward and my hands won't go up, so it's my face that lands in the rust-dust of Martian soil and then I'm gone. I'm gone.

I'm dead.

I guess I'm dead.

Or I'm not dead.

Because I can feel all my parts, I can't be dead. My tongue is loose again. I feel normal.

I feel normal, but nothing is normal. Time has done a skip and a hop.

I can't explain it, but suddenly I'm on Mars.

Finally.

Maybe Mom is right and the trip addles your brain and makes you forget and makes you confused, because this time, I open my eyes and look up and down and sideways and it's true, because it's real, and I'm on Mars. I see biomes through the glass of my helmet, a row of biomes, as well as long, low buildings with roofs that curve upward like sails. I see sky that's greenish, not orange or red or blue.

"Mars," I say, out loud, and my voice is trapped in a suit that I'm wearing, after all. I'm smiling, I'm so happy. I made it. I must have made it, because I'm here. I'm actually here. When did I come? I can't remember anything after sitting under a tree and a *crackle* and it doesn't matter because I'm here and I know which one is my biome, the one I was going toward when I tripped, so I start to walk. One foot, then the other. I'm strangely light, but stuck to the ground by my heavy feet.

("They have moments of lucidity," Mom says about her patients. "Sometimes they know exactly who they are. It's almost harder than when they don't.")

Anyway, who cares? The thing is that I'm here. I'm home. I've never felt happy like this. I've never felt so strongly that I'm in the right place, exactly the right place.

Then something makes another sound.

What is it?

It's like a bee in my suit at first. A zapping sound and a crawling feeling on my skin. It gets louder and louder. And then that crackling again in reverse. I swat at it, but you can't swat at something that is inside a suit. Are there insects on Mars? No. Think. What is it? My body is shaking, or it's being shaken. Is it an earthquake? I wish I didn't have such a bad headache.

And then, *Bam!* the scene jumps, like when you're watching a scratched DVD, and there I am on the ground under the tree and Mr. Wall — whose moustache *does* join under his chin like a giant *O* — is above me shouting something and someone (Bea?) is crying, and all around me is my whole class staring at me and then Fish-boy loudly and clearly says, "She's wet her pants!" Then there is the hushed sound of people trying not to giggle and then a laugh leaks out and then another and my mouth isn't working because of the pins in it. Why are there pins in my mouth again? Where is my tongue? Why have I wet my pants? I don't remember needing to pee.

A siren splits the air. It is so loud that it feels like it drills right through my eyes and ears like a sharp spike. I am all needles and pins, pins and needles. There are people asking me questions and taking my pulse and shining lights in my eyes. Time is jittering. Everything is too fast and too slow at the same time. I'm lifted and moved. The sheets on the stretcher are cool and smooth and I'm so so so tired, so I just smile at the people gently, kindly, like Iris, and close my eyes and think about how later, when I wake up, I'll tell them about Mars, and about how it smelled like metal and dust and something sweet like maple sugar and how the butterfly was different and so beautiful, and worth chasing out the door, and worth following into the too-bright sunlight, into the unbreathable air out there, the green sky all heavy with dust all around me.

10

I haven't been in the hospital before, but I know that I'm in a hospital because it is exactly like it looks on every hospital TV show ever. There is an IV in my arm and machines beeping around my head and, on the other side of a glass wall, my mom and dad, looking like people normally look at the top of the Tower of Terror (except without their arms in the air). I feel like a fish in a tank. A goldfish. Bubble, bubble. Ish, Fish. Fish-Ish. There should be a tipped-over treasure chest beside me or a plant to swim into or hide behind, but there isn't, and anyway, I can't move. I blink. *Tick, tick, tick.*

There is a really terrible painting of a flower hanging on an angle, like someone just remembered decorations were nice and threw it up there at the last minute. The flower is orange and droopy. Someone painted that and thought it was good. Someone looked at it and agreed and bought it.

The whole world is so dumb and sad, I can hardly stand it, honestly. I feel like crying. Not just because of the flower, but because I'm in a hospital and the dumbness and sadness of everything is totally amplified by this room. Maybe it's the smell? There is a smell in here that's worse than school, worse than anything. Antiseptic and vomit and below that, something awful and more ominous. One time, Tig and I found a dead raccoon in the woods. "I've never smelled anything dead before," he said, and we stood and breathed it in and stared. It smells like that in here. Is it me? Am I a dead raccoon? The raccoon had flies on his eyes. I try not to panic. I try to breathe slowly, in and out, in and out. My heart beat speeds up and a machine beeps faster.

The IV is dripping something purple into my arm.

Why is it purple?

Why am I here?

I try to remember, but I can't quite figure it out. My head feels funny. I blink at Mom and Dad. Why aren't they coming in here? They are looking at me but not seeing me. Blink, blink, *tick, tick, tick*. Come on Mom, why can't you hear it? I blink an SOS.

Trying to figure this out is like pedaling with a bike chain that's slipped off the pedal wheel. The pedal is still going around but not catching on anything at all. My chain did that a lot until we got it tightened. We had to go to a special bike shop. It was a two-hour drive.

"Tighten your chain," I tell myself. But I can't! I try to squeeze my brain down so my thoughts stop slipping. It's hard. It doesn't work. "Think."

I close my eyes because keeping them open is too hard and I try to go back to how it was hot and the first day of school and a boy called me Fish and laughed and I wet my pants and the tarmac was hot under my new Converse and the tree threw a long, skinny shadow on the ground and then I was on Mars. Well, dumb. Obviously that was a dream. No one just goes to Mars. It takes nine months! But only if the orbits are lined up. I have an orbit tracker and I know that if you left for Mars today — if today is still today, that is — it would take seventeen months and six days, give or take a few.

I know that it would take seventeen months and six days to get to Mars, but I don't know why I am here or why Mom and Dad can't see my blinking or why my body doesn't want to move. I try to lift my arms. They are as heavy as fallen trees.

I crunch my brain into a fist and make it flex. I try to make my brain pedal smoothly from one thought to the next.

A fish. Me. A butterfly. My biome. Home. Wetting my pants. Tarmac. Mr. Wall's *O*.

I remember eating my sandwich and lying down on the ground. I remember the tree left sticky sap in my hair. I remember Mr. Wall's beard. Something was in between the tree and the beard.

"She's wet her pants!"

It keeps playing in my head, on a loop, over and over again. I hate that boy. That Fish-boy. Who is he, anyway?

Lightning.

The tree was hit by lightning.

It crackled.

But I went to Mars, I really did. It was so different. How it smelled. How the air tasted in my mouth. That butterfly.

I *love* Mars.

I'm still on Mars.

Am I?

No, no hospitals there. No Mom and Dad.

But, I mean, look. Look around! Don't you see?

The air is still green and dusty and I'm breathing. Only I can't be breathing because ninety-nine percent of the atmosphere on Mars is made up of carbon dioxide. But wait, I'm in a suit, which is good, although I didn't put one on, so this is the dream again. I tell myself firmly, "Dream."

Wait, I'm sleeping.

Am I?

But I'm not. I can't be. I mean, I can sit up. I can sit up, so I do. Then, because I can, I stand. I walk on my heavy-light feet all the way to the dome, each foot-step feeling like it takes forever. I enter the airlock. I lift my arm and punch in a code (1430), which I somehow know and the airlock fills with pressure, like being inside a balloon that's being blown up. How could this be a dream? My skin hurts while the suit decompresses. It's a tight-loose feeling that's hard to explain.

I don't understand any of this, I just know what's real and what isn't. I lean against the airlock wall, which is cold and solid behind me until an alarm beeps, which means I can go back into the dome. I look at my hands, which is something that Dad taught me a long time ago about dreaming, but my hands are just my hands. I scratch my cheek, which is super itchy, and it's like normal, like I'm scratching my cheek. There are bumps on it. Mosquito bites. There are no mosquitoes on Mars. What? Wait. They must have changed their mind about sending twelve-year-olds to Mars because these are my regular hands. My regular nose. My three mosquito bites. My hair swings over my shoulder in a ponytail and I pull it forward and inspect it and it's my regular hair, too red, too long.

I take a deep breath and it smells green and damp and humid, like it does in my greenhouse. Crops are growing everywhere and a path of flat red rocks threads between them. At the end of the path is another door, and I make my way down the path, plants brushing my legs, and I open it. I go inside the room. Two boys are in there, playing a game of chess.

"Hey," says Tig. "Where were you?"

"I went outside," I say. My voice sounds thin and high. I clear my throat. Can you clear your throat in a dream? "I went outside," I say again. "Without a suit. I passed out. I had a dream. But then I was wearing a suit. I don't know. Just a hiccup. Brain hiccup. I guess. Mars brain?"

Tig nods. Tig is Tig, but he looks older. Is it ten years later? There's a faint beard on his chin. His eyes look like my dad's, crinkling at the corners. Is it even later than that?

"Then you'd be dead, Fish," says the other boy, who is also a man.

I squint, trying to place him. Oh. It's Fish-boy. I don't hate him now. Why don't I? I check my hands again. Maybe they are more grown-up hands. Maybe I am more grown up than I thought. But they look like my hands. Maybe bigger. Yes, I guess a bit bigger. Maybe I didn't grow so much between twelve and twenty-two. Maybe I'm really the same.

The mosquito bites bug me. Those can't be real if this is the future and I'm in it.

"I think I was hit by lightning," I say.

"No, you weren't," says Tig.

"Definitely not," says Fish-boy. "Mars brain. Remember? I'm a doctor."

"He is," says Tig. "Remember? I'm just the tech guy."

"What am I?" I say. "I don't remember. Why do you keep saying 'Remember?' I don't remember anything." I feel panicky but not too bad, like this is familiar somehow, scary but comfortable. ("You'll all beat each other up with your Mars supplies," Mom had said, but I don't feel like hitting anyone.) "Mom was right," I say.

"You're the botanist," Tig says.

"Oh, plants," I say.

"Right," he says.

"Like in the book," I say. "The one we read when we were kids. I loved that book."

"And the movie," he says. "Yeah, yeah."

"The only book that I read when I was a kid was *The Velveteen Rabbit*," says Fish-boy.

"That can't be true," says Tig.

"I mean it's the one I remember. Like if you said, 'What books did you read when you were a kid?' that's what I'd say."

"I read that," I say. "It made me cry. That rabbit just wanted to be real."

"Everyone just wants to be real," says Tig.

"You're real," I say.

"You know who I mean," he says. "Your parents."

"Don't talk about that," I say, panicking. Fish-boy doesn't know I was adopted. It's a secret! Tig said he'd never tell.

"Everyone knows," Tig says. "Remember?"

"Stop saying that!" I say.

The room has canvas floors and walls and the table they are playing chess on is a folding card table. It smells like a tent. It feels like camping. My head aches. They've made their chairs out of boxes. The boxes are labeled PROTEIN x 1000. The chess pieces look old, like Grandpa Hoppy's.

"Where did you get that?" I start to ask, but then there is a *whoosh* and a *crackle* and I'm moving. I'm moving. What's going on? I try to ask, but my mouth feels taped shut and those stupid pins. Why are mouth-pins a thing? Who put them there? I blink, hard, *tick, tick, tick*. I pinch myself. I'm alive. Am I?

"Where?" I keep saying. "Where?" But the boys are gone. The room is gone. Everything is gone.

And then I'm panicking, breathing too much and too fast. *Beep, beep, beep, beeeeeep*.

Machine! I remind myself. *You* are a machine!

The air tunnels and thickens and thins, and then I'm in the hospital and there is the crooked picture and someone is moving my bed, which is really a stretcher. And there are Mom and Dad! They are walking and we're in a hallway in a hospital and I'm on a bed that is rolling. I tug on Mom's sleeve and she turns to me, her face opening up a smile that wobbles like Jell-O, and then she says, "Jay, she's awake."

"We've got to get her to MRI, ma'am," says a voice I don't know, just as Dad is saying, "Ish, it's you, you're here, you're OK."

I can tell he's lying because his eye twitches. Dad's eye twitches a lot.

"Overhydration," Mom says, usually, but he always corrects her.

"Stress," he says. "Just stress."

I want to say now, "Your eye is twitching!" but the words fly away on blue butterfly wings. Suddenly I want to tell them something incredibly important that I just realized about being adopted. It's basically like that kid's book, *The Velveteen Rabbit*. I love them, so they are Real. They are our real parents! I want to tell Elliott so she won't be so mad anymore. I want them to know that I think they are real. I don't think they think that I think they are. That sentence has too many *think*s. I can't think. I can think. I can't.

"You're real," I try to say, but then I'm asleep again. I can't stay awake. I just can't. And I want to go back to Mars. Tig's there, and I have questions. I have a lot of questions! I try and I try but I can't seem to fall asleep deep enough to get there. It's behind a wall. I can't break through it. Or I need to be just a little bit asleep, so that I can't tell where I am, I can't see the hospital, but I can find a dream. I need a hammock. I need the cool night sky. I'm just stuck somewhere, in between. Help, I say, but I can't talk. I'm a machine, I think. I'm just a machine. I'm so dumb. I'm not a machine. I'm a person. I have a headache. It's the first day of school. I wet my pants.

What is going on? I don't know anymore. The sky was green. The butterfly was a moth. I wet my pants at school? Fish! Ish.

And then I'm gone. Somewhere black this time, a long hole that I've fallen down, tumbling and tumbling and I hope I don't land because that's going to hurt. It's not Mars. It's not anywhere. I'm just gone.

11

When I wake up, everything has changed.

Except nothing has changed. It's just something I feel, inside me. Not the outside. On the outside, it's still a hospital room. That terrible, sad, tragic flower painting is still on the wall and it's still crooked. It still stinks in here.

Mom is asleep in a chair beside my bed. It's not a regular chair. It's green and plasticky-looking, the kind that tips back, like a recliner that is practically a bed. She's snoring. I lift my hand and look at it and it looks like my regular, almost-thirteen-year-old hand. Is it smaller or bigger than on Mars?

I think it was real.

It can't be, but it was.

The major difference between my hand there and here is that here there are needles going into the vein on the back of it, dripping me full of who knows what. I almost throw up but I make myself not do it. You can't faint when you're lying down, so I guess it's a good thing that I am. The purple liquid has been replaced with something clear. It looks like water. Dad would like that, I think.

WWID? I frown. The thing is that I just don't think that Iris would ever be in this situation.

"She leads a charmed life," Grandpa Hoppy used to say about Iris. And I guess that's true. She does. Charmed people aren't lying in hospital beds. Charmed people don't have to worry about fainting when they're already lying down. Charmed people don't get struck by lightning during their lunch break at school.

The curtains on the window are open. I can see the sky. The sun is starting to rise and it's the same as yesterday except it's also completely different. It's orange and fiery and lighting up the hazy, yellow sky with its pinks and brights.

I blink back tears. I never used to cry! I am not a crier! But now I can't seem to help it. You think you know how something is going to go, like, say, the first day of school. You think you've thought of the worst possible scenarios and the best ones and all the ones in between! And then somehow none of those happen and instead you get hit by lightning, something crackles, a boy calls you Fish, and you wet your pants and wake up in the hospital with a headache that's so bad, you can feel it in your hair.

Great. I blink and blink because I'm almost crying again. Still. Blinking sounds different when your eyes are wet. It's like the tears mute the sound, like how shouting underwater never works. *Slish, slosh, slish.*

I move my head from side to side and suddenly, like magic, it stops hurting, which is weird, because now that it's miraculously not hurting, I realize that it's been hurting nonstop for a long time. Like around nine months and a week or so, from the time when Tig came over and said, "This is it, we gotta go."

And I said, "I'm going to miss you."

And he shrugged and looked somewhere beyond me, past my shoulder to the lake, and said, "I'm sure gonna miss that island."

And I'd said, "And me?"

And he laughed and said, "Yeah, sure."

And then he left. He didn't even hug me or anything. He didn't touch me at all. Not that I thought he would. Not that I wanted him to do that. But we'd spent our whole lives together! A handshake would have been nice. Weird, but nice.

The headaches started the next day.

My brain makes a small whooshing sound, like there is wind inside me. A breeze. Or someone tiny is blowing down my neck.

But it doesn't hurt. It's light. And I feel nothing.

Maybe I am nothing.

I'm airy. I'm air.

I feel like if you aimed a flashlight at this bed where I am lying, you'd see nothing but rumpled white sheets.

It's so weird. I don't know what else to say, it's just weird. It's the weirdest feeling. Everything about it is so much more than weird but there isn't a word weird enough to describe it.

"Weird," I say out loud. Even the word *weird* is weird when you toy with it enough with your tongue.

Mom wakes up suddenly and sees me. She sits bolt upright, like she's been scared out of her mind. "ISH!" she shrieks.

"Hi, Mom," I say. My words are a bit too long, like my battery is running out. "Hiiiii, . . . mooooom." (Q: What does a calf call its mother? A: Moom.)

"Oh my gosh," she says. "Ish." Then she bursts into tears. That's how I know that something really serious is happening.

Something really bad.

"I have to call your dad!" she says. She's stabbing at her phone, squinting, like in a bad dream when you're trying to call for help but every number you punch is the wrong one. She must have Dad programmed into her phone. She looks deranged.

"Mom," I say. "Your glasses?" I point at her head where her emerald green glasses are nestled in her blond hair.

"Yes, yes, right," she says, sliding them down from her hair onto her nose. They remind me of a bird, perching there for a minute but about to take off.

She puts the phone on speaker and I can hear the phone ringing and then Dad answering without saying "hello." "Is she awake?"

"She's awake," says Mom, and she's sort of crying.

Was I not supposed to be awake? I am sleepy. I feel like I could fall asleep again pretty easily. I hope they aren't disappointed if I do.

"I'm on my way," says Dad. "I'll be right there."

I close my eyes. That's nice, I think. Dad's coming! The trouble is that I'm already dreaming before I realize that I forgot to ask any of the important questions. But the dream has come up over me like a blanket, blocking out all the light, and then I'm on a bed somewhere else. A hard bed, long and narrow. I force my eyes open and look out the window and I see blackness and stars, and in the far western sky, a bright planet. Oh, that's the Earth, I think. I mean, I know it. That light in the sky is my old planet.

And just like that, I'm back on Mars, where I'm supposed to be. I close my eyes, inside the dream, and fall asleep for real, not dreaming anything at all.

It feels normal and right, like I'm a layer inside a layer, that these two things are happening at the same time. The future and the present. Which can happen, you know. Theoretically. You could exist in two places and in two times and in two dimensions at the exact same time. I forget how it works. I just know it does. It's something about strings. String theory. The physics of things. Physics is like a language I can almost understand, but not. It's like science in a dream. I just . . .

"ISH!" I hear, and then I smell my Dad's clean hands. I smell them before I can pull myself all the way out of the sleep that I'm stuck underneath. I push at it with my hands.

"Dad!" I say, thickly.

He hugs me, hard.

"Don't squash her!" says Mom.

They are both staring at me like they've never seen me before.

"What?" I say. "What?"

They look at each other. It's one of those long, starey looks that parents give to each other right before they tell you that oh, by the way, you're adopted, do you still want to go on the Tower of Terror? You can choose a T-shirt in the shop at the bottom of the ride!

"*Mom*," I say. ("Moooooom," I moo. Ha-ha.)

"Honey," she says. "I'm just going to say it. OK. Please don't panic." She shoots a look at Dad.

His eye is twitching like crazy. "You have a brain tumor," Dad blurts.

Then they both burst into tears.

I get stuck in the scene, it keeps jerking back and then rolling forward again.

"You have a brain tumor," Dad blurts.

Then they both burst into tears.

Again:

"You have a brain tumor," Dad blurts.

Then the both burst into tears.

Again:

"You have a brain tumor," Dad blurts. Then they both burst into tears.

"Oh!" I say. I smile kindly and gently, in an Iris-way.

"That's OK." I want them to feel better. Then, "I know." Which turns out to be true. As soon as they said it, I recognized it. Like I'd known all along, I just didn't want anyone else to know. The brain tumor was a secret that I pinkie swore to myself that I wouldn't tell about. I used to share all my secrets with Tig. About three months ago, I wrote on a little piece of paper "I think I have a brain tumor" and I took it to his old house and put it under a rock by the front entrance. I bet it's still there. Sometimes we used to leave each other keys under there. We never left notes, but I wish we had now. It seems like something that would have been fun that we missed out on, doing that.

Dad starts to explain exactly what kind of brain tumor I have. There are a lot of words with a lot of syllables and the syllables keep falling apart and joining together the wrong way, so I can't understand them. "Diffuse Intrinsic Pontine Glioma," he repeats. It sounds like the name of a star or a galaxy. I smile. The ancient Babylonians called Mars Nirgal, which meant Death Star. It feels important to tell Dad about that, but I can't. Did he say the word *Nirgal*? Or did I imagine it? Dad says the words again, all in a jumble of Intrinsically Pointed Nirgal Aromas. He gestures with his hands and the soap smell wafts around me like something pleasant.

I fall asleep again, instantly, without deciding. It just happens. I know that's not how many people would react to bad news, but it turns out having a tumor — a

Nirgal — in your brain is really really really exhausting.
Who knew?

Well, probably everyone, I guess.

They just hoped it wouldn't happen to them.

And lucky them, I guess, because it didn't. It happened
to me instead.

12

From the hallway, there is the clatter of dinner trays on carts and the chatter of the people who push the carts, collecting the old trays. Hospitals are noisy and, like, *raucous*. That's a word I've never used before that just came to me. I don't know why. Maybe the Death Star in my brain is causing strange loop-de-loops. Maybe I'll start speaking Japanese or understanding how to read braille.

I feel like laughing but I don't know why. It's like the laugh is coming before the punch line. What is funny out there in the hall? I can hear laughing! I think about cow jokes. If someone comes in here, maybe I will tell one.

Q: Why can't cows keep secrets? A: They just go in one ear and out the udder.

Udder is a funny word. *Udder*neath. *Udder*wear. *Udder*-wise. You get the idea. I'm pretty sure Dad's right about the cows.

Someone drops something in the hallway with a huge bang that makes me jump. The paging system comes to life: "Paging Dr. Klein, please report to Three South. Dr. Klein."

Come on, Dr. Klein! Hurry! I wonder what is on Three South. The hospital is full of people who are having just as crappy a day as I am, I guess. Maybe not, though. Maybe Three South is the good ward. Maybe it's the place where people go who are happy. I don't know why. What would they do there? What good things happen in hospitals anyway? Maybe babies are being born. I don't know where I was born. Maybe I was born in a hospital. Maybe this one. Maybe Dr. Klein's face was the first face I ever saw. It's weird how babies don't see their moms first. I guess they see the doctor or the nurse. They see a whole crowd before their mom swims into view. That's kind of sad, if you think about it. I was almost a year old when I got adopted. Whose face did I see first? Who did I used to know? I bet Elliott remembers. She was three. Three is pretty old. I think I remember things from being three. I remember a big black dog jumping on me in a park. I was carrying a red umbrella. I was with Grandpa Hoppy. He came hopping over to us and hit that dog with his cane. The dog was just being friendly though. I remember that like it's a photo in my brain, the dog wagging and Grandpa Hoppy shouting like a madman. He was quite a "character." Everyone says so.

I've seen real, actual photos of my first day with Mom and Dad, so even though I don't remember it, I sort of do, because of the pictures. I'm wearing these super-awful bright green overalls. Who puts a redheaded kid in green overalls? I look like a Christmas elf.

Mom says there was chocolate cake. She says that Elliott pushed my face into it (by mistake) and I came up crying and they knew they were in for a bumpy ride. Yeah. No kidding. After Iris, we must have been a pretty big shock.

Someone shouts. I hear running footsteps.

Things beep and kids cry and nurses open the door and swing it shut and light floods the room and then dims again and someone is always ringing something and talking too loudly and there are footsteps clicking down the hall. It's weird (again! weird!) how quickly it almost seems sort of normal to me. What should be normal to me right now is to be at home in bed, dreading school tomorrow and hoping the boy who called me Fish has suddenly been chosen to go to school in the Antarctic, where he'll likely be eaten by polar bears. Unless those are in the Arctic. I get Earth facts mixed up. I read somewhere that we won't ever really go to Mars because there are places on Earth that are pretty inhospitable (like Mars) and we seem in no rush to live there. I'm pretty sure the article referred to the Antarctic as being especially hostile. Well, I hope that's where he goes. I hope that's where he is right now, shivering and wondering, *What happened?*

Through the parted curtains, I can see the moon, which is full and bright, and above it, I can see Cassiopeia. I find the Big Dipper, which points at the North Star, which hangs there halfway in between. I wonder if any of those stars are still there or if they are just ghosts. I wonder if I'm going to die and I'll be a ghost. I wonder which ones of those dumb stars made me, and which ones of them made my tumor, because if you think about it, cancer is also made of dead stars. Everything is. Good and Bad. Fish-boy and me. Elliott and Iris. Mom and Dad. The people picking up the dinner trays. Everyone. Everything. Dr. Klein. Plastic waste! It's not just us that are dead stars. That would be too poetic and too pretty! It's all the bad stuff, too. It's all the worst stuff. You just don't see that on posters. You never will. No one will drink their coffee out of a cup that says CANCER IS MADE FROM DEAD STARS superimposed in pretty calligraphy over a crookedly painted constellation. It just won't happen.

I'm not tired at all, which is dumb because I'm always tired, but when I should sleep, I can't. I'm wide-awake. My brain is basically a salad spinner, whirling unrelated ideas. "Slow down," I tell it. "Give me a break here." It ignores me. Well, it is me. Is it possible to ignore yourself?

The doctor who was here earlier said the tumor is about the size of a Brussels sprout. "Not a kohlrabi?" I said, and I laughed.

He said, "What's kohlrabi?" But he looked so serious about it that I couldn't answer. It had seemed funny when I first said it and then it wasn't.

"Never mind," I said.

He showed me on the MRI. My brain looked like a

shadow. It looked like the censors had come along and rubbed it out so we couldn't see how ugly it really was. I imagine it covered with graffiti and misspelled four-letter words. *Bleep it*, the network would say. *That tumor is PG-13*. The tumor itself just looked like an empty space where brain should be but wasn't anymore, a blankness opening up inside of me.

Before he left, he rested his hand on my hand for a good long second or two or maybe even three. I didn't know him, so I pulled my hand out from under his. I don't much like being touched, especially not by strangers.

There were Brussels sprouts on my dinner tray and I wonder if they planned that, or if this is all a joke, after all. I hate Brussels sprouts but I ate them anyway. They were mushy and tasted like sweat and wet card-board. *Take that, sprouts*, I thought, chewing hard.

Now I'm awake. I don't know what time it is. Mom and Dad are gone for the night. I know that without remembering them leaving. Was I asleep? Half-asleep? Not paying attention? Is the tumor just erasing things willy-nilly from my brain?

The overhead light in the room has been turned off and now there's a different light that shines behind my headboard so it's never quite dark in here. I think about the hammock and how I slept in it and it left diamonds on my skin, and that was only a few days ago but it was also a different life. I think maybe if I hadn't gone to school that day, this wouldn't have happened, even though obviously it would. It's my fate. It was my Fate all along. Capital-F Fate. I want to tell Tig about it really bad. He'd know what to say. He'd know what to do. Maybe we could run away, the two of us. We could go to the Mars Now headquarters, which is in Iceland. We could explain. Mars is full of radiation. For most people, that would be bad. For me, it might save my life. That's what the doctor said. "Radiation is our first hope," he said. Mars could save me. Tig would get me there, if he knew.

I do a bit more crying. I'm not a machine. I'm not going to Mars. I'm a kid with a Brussels sprout named Nirgal in my brain, my own Death Star. Starting tomorrow, I'm going to have radiation treatments and they will shrink the sprout down to a cherry tomato and then down to a lima bean and then a green pea and then they will go in and cut out what is left if they can. My head is a salad bowl. Everything is salad.

Mom and Dad brought my laptop, so I pull it out of the drawer beside my bed and I log into the hospital wifi and check my email, more out of habit than anything.

Then I blink.

And blink again.

Tick, tick, tick.

I can't stop blinking.

The email from Tig says this:

Ish,

I bet you thought I forgot you but I didn't. I'm not good at writing emails that much. I met some kids and we've been hanging out. School is OK. I'm doing a thing about recycling that's pretty cool. It isn't the same as home but it also sort of is, if you know what I mean. I miss you and S.S. Rafty and Lunch Island. I'm sorry about that day on the island. Awkwardness is the worst. I don't know what I thought. I guess I love you. I didn't want to cry so I tried to put you away somewhere where I wouldn't think about you. It's dumb. I know it is. I made up a story that you went to Mars and left me here alone and I was so mad at you, it made it easier not to talk to you. Portland is OK. People here are kind of weird. It's raining pretty hard right now. It's always noisier here than at home. There's a lot of traffic. It's nice not to be so hot all the time. I miss the lake. Is there any water left in it? Did you read that Lake Meade is full of perchlorate? We might have been right about the lake. OK, bye for now.

Tig

I delete it and then I undelete it and then I read it again, and then I wish Mom hadn't brought in my laptop because maybe it's the radiation from the laptop that put this tumor in my brain.

Or maybe it's Tig's fault for leaving a big hole in there that cancer could fill up.

I guess I love you.

We are only twelve. Nobody loves anybody yet. Right?

I guess I love you.

I have a brain tumor.

Or maybe it was just bad luck or the way the wind was blowing one day that blew a speck of something into me that turned out to be a seed that grew.

I hit reply.

I write:

Tig,

I miss all that stuff too. Except I don't miss me. You can't miss yourself. (Ha-ha.) I miss you. I was mad you left me on Mars alone. You said you wouldn't. Your house has cracked.

Love, Ish

PS — I have a brain tumor. I've named it Nirgal.

I stare at it on the screen for a few minutes, then I delete the PS. I can't tell him. I want to. I don't know why I can't. I guess because if I do, then it becomes true.

I leave everything out that matters. I leave everything out that I meant to say. I sneak the love in there, though, just so he knows that I know. Just so he sees that I get it and that I feel it, too, even though I don't really know if it matters now at all.

13

When I wake up, it is daylight and Fish-boy is sitting beside my bed in the green vinyl chair. Naturally, I scream.

"Hey," he says. "Don't do that! Stop!"

I don't stop.

He looks afraid. "What are you doing?"

"Sorry," I say, stopping, even though I'm not sorry. What is he doing here? "What are you doing? Here, I mean. Why are you here?"

"Oh, right," he says. "Um, the class made you this card." He lifts up a huge piece of purple poster board. All over it, people have written nice things. "Get well soon! xo Kaitlyn." And "We miss you sooooooooooo much! — Amber" And "OMG, I love you and miss you! — Bea." Everything on the card looks like a lie. Do they really love me? Do I love them? I mean, it's nice if they do, but right away I feel sort of bad because if one of them had a brain tumor and wet their pants under the tree, I'm not sure if, OMG I LOVE YOU would be my first reaction. Maybe I'm a bad person. They should know this before they love me up in this way! I sigh.

"What's wrong?" he goes.

"Nothing," I tell him. Explaining would be too hard. He is not Tig, after all. I make a mental note to write Tig an email when Fish-boy leaves, explaining. He'll get it. Thank goodness he is back in my life and no longer Dead To Me. Although I'm still mad at him, so maybe he's just moved up to Comatose To Me.

I look back at the massive card because I can't not. It's blocking my view of absolutely everything else. Pictures have been cut out of magazines and glued on. (I guess Mr. Wall anticipated the need for collage-based Get Well cards when he put together the school supply list! Impressive.) There is a picture of a blue purse. There is another one of a lamb drinking from a baby bottle. There is a plate of macaroni and cheese with a fork lifting a gooey-looking bite. There is a picture of a very skinny Jesus on a cross, his mouth hanging open. Is this how people see me? It's crazy! None of it makes sense! Oh, Ish Love? She makes me think of *newborn lambs*. I mean, seriously.

In the bottom corner, Mr. Wall has written, "Our prayers are with you, Mischa. Mr. Wall." Mr. Wall doesn't look like someone who prays. He looks like someone who runs over coyotes and doesn't look back. That is one insincere-looking Get Well prayer, I think. I roll my eyes.

"Yeah," says Fish-boy. "I know what you mean. Look, this was mine." He points to a picture of a motorcycle that he's stuck a coyote underneath. The coyote's legs are sticking straight up because it's a photo of a standing coyote that he's just turned upside down.

It is hilarious, but I won't give him the satisfaction of laughing. Well, a small laugh escapes, but it's by accident.

"You don't know anything," I say, covering up my giggle. "How did you get here?"

"My mom works here," he says. "She's a doctor? She brought me. I have to go in, like, an hour."

"An hour?" I say. I feel sort of stupefied, like I can't process what he is saying. An hour is a long time. "Is she Dr. Klein?"

"Yes!" he says. He looks surprised. "How did you know that?"

How did I know? I don't know! I frown. What am I going to say to Fish-boy for a whole hour? Tears prick my eyes. I don't blink them away because I don't want him to hear them *slish slosh slish*ing.

"Um," he says. "I'm sorry I said that thing about—"

"Don't," I go. "Please don't say what you're going to say."

"OK," he says. "But seriously, I don't know why I did that. I'm not mean. I swear. I'm, like, normal. I was nervous? I'm new." When he talks, his voice has a random uptick, even when he's not asking a question. He taps his sneaker up and down on the ground. His sneaker is a hot pink Converse.

I almost laugh *again*, but then I don't. Mom would like him for a daughter, though! He's sparklier than me and Elliott put together, but that's because neither of us is sparkly.

"This is kind of awkward," he says. "I don't know you. I'm the new guy. They should have sent one of your friends, I guess."

"Yeah," I say. "For me, too." I don't tell him that Tig was my only friend. I don't want to imagine how probably no one else volunteered to come. I feel bad that I wasn't nicer to everyone. There's nothing wrong with those girls! They are perfectly nice girls! It's me. I'm the one who isn't that nice.

Fish-boy taps his hands on the arms of the chair. It's like his whole body is tapping. Maybe the tapping is an energy that all boys just have and can't help, like the hiccups. He reminds me of a boy version of Elliott, the way his whole body seems to participate in his thoughts. I think my body isn't like that. I think I hold still a lot.

"I liked that thing you were drawing," he volunteers. "In class. Like a greenhouse?"

"Thanks," I say. "It was a Mars colony." My face is burning. An hour is too long. An hour is forever. I sigh. "I don't know your name," I say. I'm trying to be polite. Even though, in my head, I keep hearing him saying, "She's wet her pants!" And "Fish!" *I don't forgive you*, I think but don't say. I might decide to forgive him. He's wearing pink shoes. He's funnier than he thinks.

"Gavriel," he says. "Gav."

"Gav," I say. "Huh."

"Yeah," he says. "My parents named me after their dog."

"For real?"

"I know," he says. "Lame, right? It's an angel, actually. Anyway, it died."

"The dog was an angel?" I ask. "The angel died?"

"No, dummy, Gavriel was an angel. The dog died."

"But Gavriel was the dog," I say. I'm being a jerk, but it's also sort of funny.

He looks at me like he can't tell if I'm kidding or not. I like people who are accidentally funny more than people who are funny on purpose. He is absolutely accidentally funny.

"The *dog* was named after an angel," he says, slowly, like I'm really dumb.

I'm trying not to laugh. "Um," I say. "I guess they loved the dog?"

"They did," he says. "He was a ..." he hesitates. "A teacup poodle."

And then I'm laughing for real and so is he. His laugh is nice, like ice in a glass of water. It's weird how things go, how I happen to be lying here with a Brussels-sprout-Death-Star in my brain, laughing with Fish-boy, of all people. But it's pretty OK, I guess.

I want to tell him about Mars and how I want to be in the first group of settlers, but I don't. It's too important.

What if he thinks I'm joking? What if he laughs? Instead, I go, "Are you missing school for this?" I wish I'd been awake when he got here. I wish I'd brushed my hair or something. I haven't had a shower in forever. I probably smell awful.

"Yep," he says, leaning back and putting his hands behind his head. "I wouldn't exactly say I'm *missing* it, though."

"Ha-ha," I say.

"I'm funny," he says. "You'll see."

"Maybe," I say. *But if you think you're funny, then you're not!* I want to say, but don't. There's a silence while we both think about how maybe I won't be alive long enough to see if he's funny or not. I might be dead. Me being dead is the elephant that shares this room with me. That's a saying: *the elephant in the room.* It's basically the huge, enormous topic that everyone avoids, but you all know it's there, you just keep your eyes averted so you can pretend not to notice it.

The thing with brain tumors is that you sometimes die. I'd never really thought about it before I got one. You just don't know.

I try to remember what we were talking about. Oh right, being funny. "Um, my dad's funny. He writes … jokes and stuff. In movies. He's working on a Martian movie that's pretty terrible, but his dream is to write one about cows. He thinks cows will be the next big thing."

"Really?" he says. "That's cool. I like cows. They

are just sort of automatically funny. Maybe he could combine them to have Martian cows. Why do we assume Martians would be personlike? Maybe they just walk around all day, mooing and grazing and chewing and stuff." He pauses and then he leans back and scratches his curly hair. I can hear his nails against his scalp. *Scritch, scratch, scritch, scratch.* Then he goes, "My dad's dead, actually."

"What?" I say. "Dead-dead?" Like there might be another, more temporary dead that his dad could be. Dead To Me, like Tig was. That's what I mean.

"It was cancer," he says, quietly. He looks past my face and out the window.

I look at the window to see what he sees, but I just see both of us, reflected in the glass.

"What?" I say, even though I heard him fine. Isn't he supposed to be cheering me up? Shouldn't he have lied or something to protect my feelings?

"Cancer," he says again, like he thinks I missed it. "Lung cancer. He didn't smoke or anything. It was just really bad luck." I roll over and push my face into the pillow so he can't see the tears that are suddenly leaking down my face.

"Oh, man," he says, "I'm sorry! I didn't mean that you're ..."

"Whatever," I say, muffled. "It's fine. I'm kind of tired."

"Um," he goes. "I still have forty-five minutes to wait for my mom."

"Well, you can sit there if you want," I say. "But I'm going to sleep."

"Cool."

I lie there, totally awake, watching a flock of brown birds fly from the top of one building to the next in a big, undulating wave. It's pretty beautiful, how they do that. How do they know where to go and who to follow? One of those birds is making the decision! One of them is thinking, "Well, time to move the troops over to the next building!" The rest are followers. But it's impossible to tell which one is leading. It's not the one at the front, it's probably one in the middle. But then how would the front ones know where to go? But if you really look, you can see that the front bird is changing all the time, slipping back into the middle, then out the back. Birds are a mystery. There are a lot of things that are a mystery. I guess I'll miss birds when I go to Mars. Buzz Aldrin and wild flocking birds and all of them.

Behind me, I hear Fish-boy tapping on the chair, then I hear the page of a book turning. The only book on my bedside table was a new copy of *The Martian* that Dad brought last night. I've read it so many times now that it's practically boring, but it's still the best Mars book that there is, if you like that kind of thing, which I do. I mean, I wish he wasn't alone on Mars for the whole book. I wish he had people with him. I wish he'd grown something other than potatoes. I wish he'd understood that the dirt he was growing them in was contaminated.

I guess if that book was real, he'd be dead of cancer before they could have gone back for him, after all.

Fish-boy coughs and then makes a super-annoying smacking sound with his lips. I shudder. I lie as still as I can and watch the birds and listen to the pages of my favorite book turning and turning. Fish-boy reads and scratches, scratches and reads and coughs. I hope he doesn't have lice and/or tuberculosis. But it's OK that he's there. It's nice. I mean, it's as nice as it's going to get with a vegetable growing in my skull in this ugly, stinky room. My skull is a biome. The cancer was the seed. Think about it. Maybe I am Mars. My brain tumor is a kid who wanted to be the first one to live there. So now I'm kind of rooting for the tumor, which is dumb. I'm Mars. Obviously, I don't want a tumor!

Eventually, I hear the click of heels on the floor and I hear Fish-boy whispering with someone who must be his mom (Dr. Klein!). I don't open my eyes. I can feel them looking at me. Then I hear them go, leaving the huge purple card lying on my legs. I wait until they're gone for sure, the door clicking back into place, before I let my eyes open again. I pick up the card again and read it to myself. "Miss you! — Zoe" "We totally miss you soooooo much already — Ana Sofia," I snort-laugh to myself, but it turns almost right away into crying, which kind of surprises me. The sadness snuck up! Why am I sad that people I usually avoid are being nice to me? I think the tumor must be in the part of my brain that used to make sense. Now nothing does. It's definitely pressing on my "cry a lot" button. I can't seem to stop. It's nuts.

I pick up *The Martian* where Gavriel, The Itchy Poodle, left it, face down on the page he was on. He didn't get very far. He must be a slow reader. (Big shock.) I start it at the beginning. I guess I'm going to have lots of time for reading in here. Anyway, reading about an astronaut who gets left behind on Mars is much closer to my dream than lying in a hospital bed, slowly realizing that this brain tumor isn't going to have a punch line and it's not going to turn out OK and somehow, suddenly, this brain tumor has just taken my whole life — my Mars future — away, blanked it out like it was never there, leaving nothing but an empty space behind.

14

I fall asleep reading, which is good, because right away, I'm in the biome. This time, I'm not working, I'm sitting. It's dark outside and I'm not alone. Someone is sitting next to me, but I can't quite see who it is. I can hear him breathing, though. Or her. I guess it could be a woman, I really don't know. We are watching the moons rising outside the glass. It's amazing. You know how sometimes, on Earth, the moon looks really huge, way bigger than normal? In this case, both moons are enormous. They also move more quickly than on Earth, so it feels sped up, like a show on fast-forward. The person next to me clears his/her throat. I keep trying to turn my head to see who it is. It's a dream, I tell myself. Just turn your head! But I can't. The dream slips away from me before I get a good grip on it. When I open my eyes, the book is still in my hand. I read until my eyes hurt and my head is aching so bad that I want to puke (again) and then the door opens to my room, the hallway sounds leaking in like a wave. I look up.

And it's the last person who I would ever have expected to see.

It's Elliott.

"Hey, Red," she goes. "Getting enough attention?"

"Funny," I say, uneasily. Is she allowed to come in here and bully me? Where are Mom and Dad, anyway?

"Mom and Dad are coming," she says. "They're just in this big boring meeting with a bunch of doctors downstairs." She shrugs. "I stayed for a while, but I couldn't stand it. Blah, blah, blah, you know?" She rolls her eyes.

"I'm sorry my brain tumor is boring," I go. "Thanks a lot."

"Cheer up," she says. "I'm here to make you feel better."

"Oh," I say. I mean, I have a lot of possible responses, such as, "Have you *ever* cheered anyone up?" or "Do you even know what that means?" She throws her long legs over the arm of the chair. She's wearing bright pink Converse. Mom must be thrilled. Maybe bright pink Converse are the Official Shoes of Cheering Up People Who Have Brain Tumors.

I want to say something, but I can't figure out how to say it. But what I'm thinking is, Oh, great, now you're going to be the daughter that Mom wishes I could *be*? But it doesn't make sense. Nothing makes sense. I open my mouth to try to say something like that, but nothing comes out.

"I'm missing cross-country practice for this," she says.

Elliott loves running. I do, too! We actually have lots in common, the more I think about it! But it's like she has no idea that I like running, she has no idea who I am, she's so busy being her.

"I didn't ask you to come," I point out. "Sorry for your terrible loss, I guess." My head is throbbing, like the brain tumor is having a party in there and invited a bunch of its friends. I picture brain tumors blossoming all over the place like Brussels sprouts on a stalk. That's how they grow, you know.

I let the silence fill up the space. Silence is better than mean stuff, at least, even if she doesn't mean to be mean. Sometimes I can't tell. She leans so far back in the chair, it nearly tips over. Her hair is starting to grow out, so even though it's mostly gray, it's this really pretty golden blond at the roots. I wish I had blond hair. Maybe I just hate Elliott because she's everything that I'm not. I mean, Iris got all the good genes (obviously not the same gene pool at all), but Elliott kind of did OK, too. She's pretty, athletic, shimmery blond, and totally OK with being herself even when she's awful. I think that last thing is the thing I envy the most. I mean, who likes themselves *all* the time? I sure don't. It seems really unfair that she got "self-confident" and I got "brain tumor."

I hate myself for thinking that, but only a little.

After what seems like forever, while I watch saline drip from the IV bag into the tube above my bed and then run down into my arm, Mom and Dad show up. It's the longest Elliott has ever gone without hurting my feelings, but that's mostly because she wasn't saying anything. Still, maybe we should call Guinness and enter it into their famous book of records! Is Guinness an actual person?

I guess even Elliott feels really bad that I'm sick, that I have cancer, that I might die. I wonder if she'll cry if I do. I am, after all, her only "real" relative. My eyes start to well up again. Lame.

"Hi, honey," says Dad, kissing me, and putting a stuffed toy under my arm.

"Hi, Dad," I say. "Thanks." I pull the toy out and look at it. It looks like a worm or an amoeba. It's brown. "What is it?"

"Oh," he goes. "It's an Ebola virus."

"You bought me an Ebola virus?" I say. "What? Why?"

"Worse than a brain tumor!" he says. "Think about it."

"Um," I say. "OK. Ha-ha." I stick the Ebola under the back of my neck. It feels nice there, soft and pretty supportive. "Thanks."

"Well, I tried," he says. "They didn't have brain tumors, anyway. I think there's some kind of disease-ism going on. I'll try to find someone to sue. Now I've got to get this one to school."

The way he says "this one," that's what a real dad would say. Elliott is so blind. She can't see love even when it's being directed right at her! I've been thinking a lot about love, I guess, while I've been lying here. I've been thinking about how people think that love is something to do with your heart when obviously it's all in your brain. Maybe my tumor is a love tumor. It's made me deficient in knowing how to love people or something, especially in that "OMG I LOVE YOU!" way that most girls my age can do. Maybe I do it wrong.

Maybe Elliott does, too, but her wrong is different from my wrong. It's another thing we have in common. I should make a list and email it to her. I don't know if she'd read it, but I want her to know that maybe we aren't so different, after all.

"I love you," I say now. I don't know if I'm talking to Elliott or to myself. Both, I guess.

"What?" she says.

"Nothing," I say.

"OK," says Elliott. "Whatever. Later, Red."

I hold my hand up in a wave, but she's already halfway out the door.

"I'll be back!" calls Dad.

"Bye, Daddy," I say. I never call him Daddy anymore. I don't know why that slipped out.

Mom takes Elliott's place in the green chair. She slides it closer to the bed and it makes a terrible *screeeeeeech, screeeeech* sound. I shiver. She smells like coffee and Cinnabon.

"Mom," I go. "Did you have Cinnabon?"

She smiles. "No!" she says. "I swear I didn't! Oh, OK. You caught me. I had a cinnamon bun. But it wasn't even good. Definitely not a Cinnabon. Just some cheap copy from the cafeteria." She leans forward. "It was stale," she says, like she's telling me a state secret. I nod, seriously.

"Good information, Mom," I say. "But that stuff is still terrible for you."

I yawn. Sleep is always lurking around me now, waiting for me to fall into it.

I'm drifting, but she talks to me anyway. She tells me that Iris is coming home in a few weeks. Iris! I'm so happy! See what I mean about Iris? Just knowing she is coming home has made everything suddenly lighter. She's helium and we are all balloons just waiting to be filled by her Irisness.

Mom says she's going to make her famous chocolate zucchini loaf and freeze some. She talks about how the weatherman said maybe it was going to rain soon and how someone must have got tired of seeing the long grass at the Diazes' old house because when they drove by this morning, it was mowed. She talks and she talks and she talks. She doesn't say anything about what the doctors said. I want to ask, but I can't. My tongue is too tired. I fall asleep and wake up and then the orderly comes into the room and says, "It's time, honey!" And I'm wheeled down to a different room for chemotherapy. I don't know what I thought chemotherapy was like but this definitely isn't it. There is a row of La-Z-Boy recliners and kids in two of them. One of them is playing an Xbox. One is watching a movie, but he has headphones on and his eyes are shut.

"You might get sleepy," the nurse says. "Most people do the first time. We put lots of Benadryl in there."

I nod. I squeeze Mom's hand and hug my Ebola tightly.

Mom smiles at me, but I can see the tears shimmering in her eyes, wanting to spill over. Her voice is as crumbly as the dry leaves at home when she says, "Want to play Monopoly?"

Monopoly stopped being my favorite game after the Great Nostril Incident of 2012, but I don't want to explain or even tell her why it makes me sad that she doesn't remember that, so I just say, "No thanks." I just want to be here and to feel this, but at the exact same time I don't want to be here. I want to be anywhere but here! I feel like inside me there is all this stuff going on: me vs. cancer; life vs. death; happy vs. sad. Sad is winning, just FYI.

"OK," she says. "We can just sit and talk if you feel like it. Or I can read to you out loud."

I shrug. "I don't know yet, Mom."

The nurse attaches the bag to the port on the back of my hand, and almost right away, there's a hot rush of something into my veins. It feels like the start of an unstoppable mistake, like leaning just a tiny bit too far off a cliff. I can sense my whole body going, "Stop! It's poison!" I can practically feel my cells recoiling.

"Sorry, cells," I say out loud.

They have to almost die so that the cancer dies. That's the game. The doctors see how close they can get to killing the patient without killing the patient. At least, that's what I heard when I read between the lines of what the doctor actually said. He's a nice man. When he smiles, wrinkles flow outward from his eyes like the cracks that formed around the beaches of the lake.

What he actually said was, "We annihilate the cancer. It's like a video game, but with your cells. Do you play Astrosmash?" Then he'd laughed and said, "I guess not, unless you also time travel back to the 1980s! I should figure out what today's equivalent is to that."

"Angry Birds?" I offered, even though I don't play it. Tig used to like it, though.

"Hmm," he said. "Do the Angry Birds blast the enemy clear out of the sky?"

I thought about it. "Not really," I said.

"Well, think about it as Angry Birds attacking the enemy and shrinking it down until it's nothing, until it's smaller than birdseed, and then . . . eating it."

"Eating it? You're going to eat my brain tumor? Poor Nirgal!"

He'd laughed, bending over at his stomach, like it was the funniest thing he ever heard. "Nope," he said. Then, "Who is Nirgal?"

"Never mind," I said. The idea of trying to explain Nirgal seemed too big to try to take on just then.

"OK," he'd said, simply, and left it at that.

Anyway, I figured out what he meant. The medicine is an angry bird. The tumor is going to get attacked, midflight, and they'll take it down. But the tumor is part of me, so I guess I just have to hope that *I* keep flying. Maybe that's where the whole metaphor falls apart. There's no "me" in Angry Birds. There are just the birds and the pigs and that's it.

I wriggle around in my chair. Mom is flipping through a magazine and the pages shimmer in the light. They look like wings. Butterfly wings. My head aches. I don't want to cry but it's sneaking up on me again. I squish my eyes shut.

I'm itchy, but not on my skin, below that, somewhere inside. Like I'm an onion and it's not the papery outer layer that's the problem, but one or two below that. There's a taste in my mouth that's like sweet pennies. Even my eyes feel weird and wrong. I try to imagine all that hot, itchy medicine as birds. I try to picture the medicine-birds flocking to the Brussels sprout and surrounding it, pecking it smaller and smaller until, eventually, it's just gone, it vanishes in the hot soup of me.

"Iris says that she's got a chance to enter a competition for her designs," Mom says. "She says that she'll bring her book and show you what she's done so far. She said to tell you that it's Martian chic or Mars-influenced or, well, something Marsish."

I smile a little bit. I don't know what that means, not really. EVA suits? Purple somethings, like in Dad's movie? Rust-colored everything?

"How do you feel?" she asks. She looks worried.

My face must look funny or something. I nod. I can't really talk. I don't know how the medicine feels. Not exactly. I *do*, but I can't say. It feels weird, I want to say. It feels *wrong*. It's nothing like Angry Birds, it's more like a flood, a wave, a *whoosh* of wrongness. But I just nod and smile, my best gentle Iris smile.

Here's what it feels like: Like my body is Lake Ochoa, dried out and too hot, sloshing in an earthquake, and everything is too dry and itchy and the sun won't quit. I feel like water on fire. We are made of water, you know. Like cucumbers. Like everything.

"If you're not OK, you should say," she says. "Can you talk?"

"I'm OK," I croak. "Iris is coming. S'nice." I don't know why my words are thick like gravy, but the Brussels sprout is hurting so bad. The chair is vibrating. It's a massage chair. I look around until I find the button that turns it off. It's better without the sloshing. The hands on the clock are moving in slow motion, like at school, but worse. I feel a tiny bit panicky. How long does this go on for? I forgot to ask. But I can't quite form the words because I'm already mostly asleep. "Bye Mom," I want to say, but it comes out in a white cloud. I think maybe I raise my fingers and wave, but maybe not.

"One comma two exclamation point One comma two exclamation point And through and through carriage return The vorpal blade went snicker hyphen snack," Mom says.

I'm being pulled into a vacuum, there's something slamming into me, what is it? The vorpal blade! Wind, sand. I can't see. It's everywhere. I'm flattened against something solid. I think it's a vehicle that I'm trying to get into, so I feel around until there is a handle and I pull and slide in. Inside, it's dark. I know it's a dream, but it doesn't feel like a dream, so what's the difference, anyway?

I'm really cold. The air has hard edges, there's a smell of ice. I start up the vehicle, I don't know how I know how, but I know that if I question stuff, I'll get confused, so I let myself drive to a building. Outside the building, there is a keypad and somehow I get out of the vehicle and punch in the code. A door lifts up and I drive the vehicle through it, as though it's a Martian car wash. My heart is beating fast. I know what I'm doing! But I don't. I want to go home. I've never thought that before. I mean, home to my house in Lake Ochoa. I start to cry. This isn't a dream, because I'm crying. Snicker-snack.

I push open the airlock door. There they are, Tig and Gavriel and some other people who I know but I don't know.

"SURPRISE!" they yell.

It's my birthday. Is it? It's my birthday! And they are hugging me and kissing me and there's a cake or something that looks sort of like a cake and I cut the cake and I make a wish and my wish is to go home and just after I blow out the candles, Tig leans over and kisses me. He kisses me!

Gavriel the Fish-boy says, "Here, this is your present. It's about what really matters. It's about what's real." He passes me a book. It's *The Velveteen Rabbit*. An old copy. He definitely brought it from Earth.

I hug him. I'm acting like a normal person who knows how to love people back! It's a miracle. I like this version of me, even though I'm not quite sure it's me. "OMG, I LOVE YOU," I say. "I mean, I love it. This. Thank you."

He laughs. "Don't worry about it. Happy twenty-first!"

I'm *twenty-one*? The mission must have left a year before schedule. How did I get picked? I really want to know!

A girl who I don't recognize gives me a hug. "Love you, Ish!" she says, like this is a normal thing to say, that people would say to each other.

"Me, too," I say. I have this feeling of incredible warmth and belonging. Like this is where I'm meant to be, always, where I've always been meant to be, like I'm home.

I'm blushing and happy and my face is hot from the candles and the blushing and then with a *whoosh*, I'm awake again. It's like that, like being thrown through space and time and I'm freezing and shivering and I'm in a chair and a few seats away, a kid is building a space-ship on Minecraft and my mom is deeply engrossed in something on her iPhone (probably Facebook, she's *always* on Facebook) and a nurse walks by and winks at me and says, "Not much longer now, sweetheart. You're doing great. In the home stretch!"

I give her a half-nod, half-yawn. The clock has sped

up. It's almost over. And I feel OK! I feel almost fine. Well, not fine. Groggy. But nothing terrible is happening. Nothing big, like what I'd expected. I don't know what I'd been expecting, actually. I guess I mostly expected never to be having chemo in Lake Ochoa Children's Hospital. I never expected *this*. Not any of this.

"Mom," I say, and she looks up and smiles.

"Good sleep?" she says, dropping her phone into her purse.

I shrug. I feel annoyed with her but I'm not sure why. For not just staring at me while I was sleeping? For not making sure I was still here?

"Not exactly," I say. I want to tell her about the dreams and about how they all snap together like pieces of LEGO to make a bigger thing, but I don't know what it is yet, or I won't know until the last piece is done. I don't know how to tell her that it feels more real than this. I touch my lips. Dumb. Stupid. No one kissed them. No one will ever kiss me. What if I die before I kiss a boy? I'm not even the kind of girl who thinks about stuff like that! Why am I thinking that now? It doesn't make any sense! The Brussels sprout is confusing my ideas about love, that's just a fact.

I guess I love you.

Nirgal loves me, in a Brussels sprout way. Without me, it's nothing, right? Without me, Nirgal doesn't exist. Or maybe *I'm* Nirgal. I rub my temples. I'm so confused. *Stop thinking*, I command myself. Thinking hurts.

Somewhere in the corner of the room, a big screen is showing the weather. A dark cloud is superimposed over all of Lake Ochoa on the map. "A hundred percent chance of significant rain," the man is saying. Someone starts to clap and then someone else, and then, before you know it, there we are in the chemo room, all of us clapping, even the Minecraft kid, who has put down his controller just for a second.

But I can't help thinking that if rain is the miracle, then maybe the only available miracle has been wasted, and it's not going to be spent on my Brussels sprout! Not that miracles work like that, but I don't really know how they *do* work. Or if I believe in them. And what if there are only so many to go around?

Mom gets up and rushes to the window and pulls back the drapes. "Look!" she says. "Look!" And just as she says it, the skies open up and rain starts to pour down, making the window a piece of art, rivulets of water everywhere; it makes it look like the glass is melting. The sound is deafening on the roof. I'd forgotten how loud rain could be, or maybe it's because we're all just quiet, staring at it, like it's everything we've been waiting for, this whole time.

15

After radiation, I get to go home. Radiation was easy, compared to chemo. I just lay there, very still. There was a humming sound, but it felt like nothing. I felt like nothing. I think I fell asleep. It hurt when they tattooed the targets onto my head, though, shaving tiny little spots on my scalp. I looked at my long red hair falling to the ground and I felt panicky, like I wanted to grab it and glue it back on. But once they were done, you couldn't even see the places unless you looked for them. They were hidden by all my other hair. I guess it's a good thing I have so much of it, after all.

"Are you sure?" I keep asking Mom. "Are you sure I can go home?" I feel like my Mars birthday wish came true! But it also feels wrong to leave the hospital with a Brussels sprout still in my brain. Shouldn't I stay until it's gone? I thought you got sent home from hospitals when you were better, not when you were really still the same, but itchier and queasier.

"I'm sure," she says. "You'll be fine at home. We come back for long chemo treatments once a week, and after school every day for radiation. If you want to go back to school, that is. Either way, radiation is every day."

"I don't want to go to school!" I say, quickly. "I can't."
"We can talk about it at home," she says, but I know
she means I don't have to go. She'd probably let me do
anything I want right now. I could say, "I want to go to
Hawaii!" and she'd take me. But I don't want to go to
Hawaii. I feel too much like throwing up.

I roll up the big purple card and put my laptop into
my backpack. I stuff the Ebola into the front pocket and
the new copy of *The Martian* in with my computer. Mom
already packed up my clothes and she's brought me clean
jeans and a white T-shirt and my orange coat. I wait for
her to pull the curtain, and then I quickly change out
of the gown. There's a bandage on the back of my hand
where they pulled the IV out. I can't explain why, but it
feels safer to stay in this ugly, smelly room.

I never used to be scared of stuff. I wasn't even scared
to go to Mars! But my hands are shaking now. I stuff
them into my jeans pockets to hold them still. I'm brave!
I'm the bravest! This is silly. I hold my head very still,
trying to not roll the Brussels sprout around too much,
like maybe all this movement is making the sprout nudge
the "scared" center of my brain. Maybe it's woken up all
my fear at once. "I can't be scared," I say out loud. "I'm
going to Mars."

Mom takes my backpack and holds the door open for
me. The corridor is empty and quiet, for a change. I stop
at the nurses' desk. "Good-bye," I tell them. "Thank you."

I don't actually recognize any of them. Maybe these are the wrong nurses. Maybe my nurses are all on their days off, at home, watching the rain fall on their dead grass.

They are nurses, though, so they are very kind even if they have no idea who I am. "Bye, sweetheart," they say. Maybe if I don't get to go to Mars, I'll be a nurse instead. I'll "sweetheart" everyone and "honey" them until they forget that they're sick. My words will hold them up like a hug from someone who loves you.

I guess I love you, I want to say to them, but I don't.

We're just getting into the elevator when a woman comes rushing up, red hair flying, a stethoscope around her neck. "Hang on!" she says. "Are you Mischa?"

"Yes," I say. For one fleeting second, I feel like she's going to say, "I'm your real mother!" I guess because she has red hair. Not very many people around here do, except for me. Instead, she goes, "I'm Gav's mother! We met, but you were asleep, I think."

I nod because I'm not sure what to say.

"He was going to come and see you again tomorrow," she says. "But you're leaving."

I nod again.

Mom must sense the awkwardness, because she jumps in. "He can come by the house!" she trills, like naturally I must be thrilled to my spine about the idea of Fish-boy coming to my house.

I try very hard to signal her with my eyes. Two blinks

means no, obviously, right? *Tick, tick*. But she doesn't seem to get it.

"We'd love to see him! You moved into the Munros' old place, right? By Haven Lane?"

"Yes!" the woman says. "Oh, how rude, I didn't introduce myself. I'm Anastasia Klein."

"It's nice to meet you, Dr. Klein," Mom says, forgetting to introduce herself back. "But we've got to get this one home to rest! Tell Gavriel we'll see him tomorrow."

I open my mouth to protest, but nothing comes out. It just opens and closes, like the goldfish that I am. "Glub, glub," I say, but no one is listening.

In the car, I try to explain. "Mom, I hate Gavriel."

"You do?" She turns the radio off. "Why?"

"*Mom*, you don't understand anything." I don't want to tell her about the way he said, "Fish." I don't want to tell her how he said, "She's wet her pants!" I can't. It's too humiliating. I reach over and turn the radio back on and then turn it up, loud. It hurts my head, but not as much as thinking about Gavriel coming to my *house*. Even if he's a bit funny, I can't forgive him for "Fish." I can't forgive him for "She's wet her pants!" It's unforgiveable. It's two unforgiveable things that, together, equal "unforgiveable forever."

"I just thought" — she turns the radio off again — "that it would be good for you to have another friend now that Tig is —"

I gasp, outraged. "You thought that because he's a boy,

he can just be Tig 2.0? You're gross, Mom. I wasn't friends with Tig BECAUSE he was a boy, I was just friends with him because we were friends! That's all! Besides, we're friends again now. He wrote to me. So there. So I don't need a new friend. I don't *need* some weird, mean boy coming over to stare at me while I'm throwing up into a bag."

"But you don't have any friends who are girls," she forges on, grimly. "A new friend right now would probably be a good thing! I'm glad to hear that Tig wrote to you! What did he say? But still, more friends is never a bad thing. You and Gavriel can be friends as *well* as your being friends with Tig."

"WE ARE NOT FRIENDS, PERIOD. And it's none of your business what Tig said. It's between me and Tig. So *stop*." I turn the radio back on, but this time I keep my hand over the knob so she can't turn it off again. The sun is blindingly bright and the sky is endless blue and the music gets into my headache and wraps around it like vines and squeezes. The one rain shower we had didn't do any good at all. Everything out there is just as dry as before, nothing has changed. Except me.

I close my eyes. My stomach is churning, bubbling, rising.

"Mom," I go. "*Mom!*" But I guess she doesn't hear me over the sound of the loud music. I throw up all over my jeans and my white T-shirt, but luckily not on my NASA jacket. It's way too hot for that here on Earth. It's way too hot for everything.

Mom pulls over, fast, cutting someone off. There's a squeal of brakes and honking. I open the door and practically fall out, throwing up and throwing up and throwing up and throwing up. My barf runs into the dry, cracked earth like it's the only thing that can save it, filling up all the crevices with everything that was ever inside me. Maybe I imagined the rain. Maybe it didn't even happen.

"You're welcome," I tell the ground, when I'm done. Mom is rubbing my back. "Don't touch me," I say. "Please don't."

So she stops. Which makes me feel mad. *Don't stop when I say stop!* I want to tell her, but how can I make that make sense?

We get into the car. We drive the rest of the way home with all the windows open, the smell of puke and death everywhere, and my mouth bitter with the taste of everything I've lost. Mom doesn't turn the radio back on. She doesn't sing. We just stare straight ahead. We both probably want to say all the right things, but we don't know how, or what the right thing even is.

16

Gavriel shows up ten whole days later. What a great "friend." (Those are ironic air quotes, in case you didn't guess that.) Ten days that I'd spent throwing up, getting radiated, sleeping dreamless days away. Ten days that I spent writing emails to Tig and not sending them. Ten days of hitting Send/Receive on my email only to get nothing back except junk mail and jokes from Iris that carefully avoid any mention of the C-word. Ten days of Elliott not asking me how I am. Ten whole days of crying and crying and crying. I've cried enough to refill the whole lake with my tears, for goodness' sake. But the lake level is still super low and the weather is still too hot and Dad is still telling Dad-jokes and drinking water and ten days doesn't change anything but it also changes everything. It's pretty much erased how funny Gavriel was in the hospital. But it hasn't erased "Fish." It hasn't erased "She's wet her pants!"

Now he is standing in my bedroom doorway, shifting awkwardly from foot to foot. I swallow acid and madness.

I have my sketch pad open on my lap, so I start to sketch him, just because. I draw arrows. "Ugly hair" I write, with an arrow. "Blank expression." I use my best scientist/explorer handwriting. Perfect capital letters that look practically like a computer did them. I draw an arrow to his armpits. "Boy-smell," I write, even though it isn't true. I can't smell him from here. He probably smells fine. It's a metaphor, that's all.

"Mom said I had to come," he offers.

I'm on my bed, fully dressed. The curtains on my Mars pictures are moving a little in the hot breeze that's blowing through the open (real) window. It makes it look even more real. I look at him looking at the wall of "windows." I try to see if he thinks it's dumb or not.

"Sorry," he mumbles.

I'd feel bad for him if I wasn't so mad. I shrug. I'm not sure what he's sorry for. For not coming sooner? For looking at my wall? "You came," I say. "Now you can go, I guess."

He steps closer. Now I can smell him. He smells like water. That's weird, but it's true, so there you have it.

"I can't," he says quickly. "Mom said I have to stay for, like, at least an hour."

"Are you on house arrest?" I go. "Is this your civic duty? Penance? What is with your mom and 'an hour'?"

"I don't know," he says. He frowns. "She does sort of do that a lot. An hour of homework. An hour of reading before bed. I guess she likes hours for some reason."

"What did you do?" I ask.

"What do you mean?"

"To be punished for an hour."

He shrugs. "Nothing," he says. Then he almost smiles. "Well, maybe some stuff."

"Fine, don't tell me, then."

"OK, I won't."

"Suit yourself."

"I like your room," he says. "Mars, huh."

"Yep," I say. "Mars."

"I'm pretty into that stuff, too," he says. "I've been Googling since I read that book in your hospital room. Mars Now is a private project that's going to go before NASA even. Have you heard of it?"

I give him the stink-eye. "Yeah," I go. "I have."

"Mars looks cool," he says. "The way they talk about it being a new society and stuff. Terraforming. I think I'd be scared to go, though. You can't come back very easily. You can't change your mind. Anyway, I'm going to be a doctor when I grow up."

"You probably would be scared," I say. "But they need doctors on Mars, too." I squint at him, remembering my dream. I don't think it was a dream. I should stop being mad at him, because I think he's going to be one of my best friends. I know that he's going to go to Mars. I can't tell him that, though! He'd think I was nutty.

He clears his throat. "Can I sit down or something? I feel, um, weird just standing here."

I give him the stink-eye until I'm sure he's noticed that I'm doing it. Being so mad is exhausting, it's like always being clenched like a fist, but inside. I sigh. "Fine."

Iris is coming home tonight. I wanted to be getting ready for Iris, but I didn't know what to do to get ready except stop throwing up. When Gavriel showed up, I was sipping tiny amounts of ice water. If I gulped, I barfed. It had to be such a small amount that it barely wet my mouth. My room probably stinks like throw-up, I realize. I look at him to see if he's making a face. I would. What is he doing here? Who is he to me? I don't have friends. He isn't my friend. I have Tig! *I guess I love you.*

"So," he says. "You're not missing anything at school."

"I know," I say. "I don't care, anyway. I don't have to go. My mom said. Having cancer trumps school, it turns out. So I win. Ha-ha." It's a fake laugh. I actually say the *ha* and the *ha*. Obviously, cancer is not funny.

"Oh," he says. "I guess you do? In a weird kind of way. Anyway, Kaitlyn and Bea got into this huge fight, like with fists and stuff. Now the whole class is either Team Kaitlyn or Team Bea."

"Wow," I say.

"Want to know what it was about?"

"Nope."

"I'm Team Bea," he says. "I don't really know either of them, but she was kind of right."

I shrug. "OK." I think about Kaitlyn's *hee-haw* laugh. "I guess I'd be Kaitlyn," I say. But then I remember how Bea was crying when I had my seizure. She's probably a better person than Kaitlyn. Kaitlyn definitely *hee-haw*ed when I wet my pants. "I don't care about those girls."

"How come you don't have a best friend?" he says. "Why do you hate everyone? No one says bad stuff about you. They all want to *make* things for you. Raise money to buy you, like, a pony or a trip to Disneyland or a cure or something."

Instead of answering him, I stare right through him. I make his molecules disappear with my eyes. I take a tiny tiny tiny sip of water, the amount a bird would take in its tiny beak. An Angry Bird. Just enough. Through the wall between my room and Elliott's, I can hear the beat of her music, which she's listening to on headphones. She'll probably be deaf before she grows up. Sad. But not really, because she's Elliott.

Gavriel breathes too loud. His breathing fills up the whole room.

Downstairs, I can hear Buzz Aldrin squawking. Sometimes he gets going and doesn't seem to remember how to stop. Or maybe he just suddenly realizes he's in a cage, he's always been in a cage, and he's pretty much trapped forever. Maybe Buzz Aldrin has the equivalent of what Mom's dementia patients have. Maybe he's yelling, "I left something burning back at the nest!" Maybe he thinks he's just waiting for a ride back to the Amazon rain forest or wherever he came from, right after he gets out of that cage.

Fish-boy tips back in my desk chair and then rights himself and then he does it again. And again. He's probably going to break it. I take another tiny, microscopic sip of water. The chair falls over and crashes to the ground and he hits the floor hard. I try not to laugh, but I do anyway.

"Not funny," he says from the floor, but he's grinning.

"I'm tired," I go. "You can stay here, but I'm going to sleep."

He shrugs. "OK," he says. "Can I read your book again?"

"Fine," I say. I take it out from under my pillow and pass it to him. I read it again last night, instead of sleeping, and this time it was different to me. It made me feel sad. It made me feel lonely. It made me not want to go to Mars. I can't tell Gavriel that, though. He probably wouldn't get it.

I lie back on my bed and close my eyes. Ever since I started chemo, my Mars dreams have gotten even weirder and more intense. Mom says I talk in my sleep. I don't think Gav would tell—he's always super nice on Mars—but I don't want to give him anything to take back to the class to say about me, just in case. I picture them all laughing, heads bent together. I'm so mad at them for all being healthy. It isn't fair. Plus, I'm mad at them for being nice to me when I don't think I deserve it. I'm mad for every reason.

I close my eyes, but I stick my thumbnail hard into the palm of my other hand, to stop myself from sleeping for real. I lie for ages with my eyes shut, listening to him tip that dumb chair, listening to him turning those pages, listening to his loud breathing. I don't even open them when I hear my inbox ping with a message, and then another one. I just ignore it. I play dead. I mean, maybe I'll *be* dead soon enough, so it's pretty stupid to waste alive time on it, but I do it anyway. It's just easier than everything else. It's the easiest choice to make. Dad used to always say, when one of us had a huge problem about something, "Water always flows downhill." I think what he meant was sometimes you should just do the easiest thing, though actually I don't think he has the saying quite right.

When the hour finally ends, Gav gets up and clears his throat. "See ya, I guess," he says.

And I go, "I guess," even though it totally blows my cover and now he knows that I was just pretending to be asleep all along.

17

As soon as he leaves, I fall asleep in a hard crash, like my laptop when something goes wrong. It's not a fade to black, it's just instant blackness. I'm back on Mars and the moon Phobos is still in view, even though it's so high up that we have to lie back to see it. Deimos is out of sight. Even as I watch, Phobos starts to split apart.

"Do you see that?" I say to the person next to me. My voice doesn't want to come out right, but I somehow make the words sound like more than whistles.

"Duh," says Elliott.

"Elliott?" I say, confused. "What are you doing here?"

Then, just like I've been rebooted, my eyes fly open and I'm awake again. Somehow I am on the couch. I don't know how I got to the couch or when I came here. I think about asking, but then I decide not to. It seems scary to be somewhere and not remember getting there. Dad is watching the news on the TV. The weather reporter is saying that it's flooding in Portland. It's a state of emergency! The water is knee deep in the streets. There is footage of a Walmart, with water in all the aisles, random items floating in it. It looks like the Apocalypse.

Dad watches with me for a few minutes and shakes his head. "Isn't it something," he says. "Never rains but it pours. Or, in some places, it just never rains."

"Uh-huh," I say. I stare at the screen intently, squinting, to see if, in the background somewhere, I'll see Tig. I don't want to miss seeing him, if he's there.

They show a middle school, which is closed and deep in the water. "Schools are closed," the reporter is saying. In the background, a group of boys splashes through the water on bicycles.

"They're going to ruin those bikes," Dad says.

I pick up the remote control and hit pause and rewind it a few seconds, then pause again. None of the boys are Tig.

"Wish they could send us their rain," Mom says, coming into the room. "The lake needs a refill!"

Our eyes all drift to the window, where we can see how low the lake has gotten. It's pretty bad. Well, it's been bad all along.

That's how we all are, that's what we're all doing, when the front door flings open and Iris comes running into the room. Iris! I'm instantly happy. She's smiling her Iris-smile and she smells like Iris and right away, she jumps over the back of the couch and gathers me up in this huge hug. "Ish," she says. "What is going on? How are you feeling?"

All I can do is blink at her and hug her back.

There's this one mountain on Mars — well, there

are lots of mountains on Mars, but one in particular —
that's called Olympus Mons. It's three times bigger than
Mount Everest. It's so huge that if you were standing
in front of it, you wouldn't be able to see the top. You'd
have to be miles away to see it. It's so big, you can't even
imagine it when you think about mountains on Earth.
Anyway, that's how I feel about Iris compared to how
I feel about everyone else. My love for Iris is Olympus
Mons.

Iris's being home changes everything. We are all talking at once and laughing and hugging and there are
plates clattering on the counter and Elliott even agrees to
play Pictionary with us after dinner. We play and nearly
die laughing at the way Dad draws pretty much everything (it all looks the same!) and at how Mom can't ever
guess even the dumbest things like "chair" or "cow." It's
the best night of my whole life. The best night ever.

I fall asleep with my face in the bowl of potato chips,
though. Nothing's perfect, I guess. I get super tired, super
fast! There's nothing I can do about it. They say that
your body does a lot of its healing while it's asleep. Let's
hope that's true.

Then, on the first day after Iris comes home, the sky
grays up, thick and heavy. It's like she brought the rain
with her. Everyone is holding their breath. "Is it going
to rain again? For real, this time? Is it?"

Even I can't take my eyes off the sky, just in case it
starts. I go out and lie in the hammock, half napping,

half waiting. I want it to rain so bad. I can feel how much the lake wants the rain, how the trees are curling their leaves up toward the hopeful sky. But instead of being a relief, it's making me really sad. I don't know why, but it is. Maybe the Brussels sprout has spread into the part of my brain that makes everything sad and is resting there, gently, like a person leaning against a wall in the shade.

I sniffle a bit and let the hammock stop swinging. I hear footsteps on the deck, so I turn my head carefully to see who it is. I always have to be careful when I turn my head now because, if I do it too fast, I get dizzy and the pain falls from one side of it to the other, like a ball dropping in a cup. I hate how it feels.

It's Elliott. I think about pretending to be asleep, but it's too late.

She goes, "The air smells like rain, even."

Elliott's barefoot and wearing old cut-off jean shorts and a T-shirt of Dad's that practically comes to her knees. Her hair is sticking up all over. We both stare at the sky.

Then for some reason, I say, "Why do you care if it rains? It's not like you care about the lake or the trees or anything."

Elliott sits down next to me, so hard that I'm practically ejected from the hammock. She stares at me. "You're pretty mean to me, you know," she says quietly. "I'm trying to cut you slack because you have cancer or whatever, but I have feelings, too."

I'm kind of taken aback. I mean, obviously Elliott has feelings. But … does she? She's so hard and tough, like one of those insects that have their skeleton on the outside. I don't know what to say, so I shrug.

"Well," Elliott says. "It would be OK if you stopped for a while. I'm trying to be nice to you." She blinks, like she's about to start crying. "I don't want you to die."

"I'm not going to die," I mumble. I lie still and cross my hands over my chest, like I'm already dead, to try it on for size. It doesn't feel good. "I'm fine."

"You have a brain tumor!" she says. "You aren't fine."

"Um, that's very reassuring," I say. "Thanks."

"You know what I mean!" she says. "Stop trying to make everything I say into something bad!"

"I'm not!" I say. "But most stuff you say *is* bad! Why do you hate me anyway?"

"I don't hate you!" she says. "You're just always mad at me!"

"I'm not!" I yell. "You're always mad at ME!"

We look at each other. We actually have the exact same color eyes. Looking at her eyes is like looking at myself, but without all the freckles and red hair to distract you. Her eyes make me think of the lake, but when it was full of chemicals. I decide not to say that bit out loud.

And then it starts to rain. It's just a few drops plopping down at first, but big drops, like tiny packages of water being sent to the Earth from space. They splatter in a pattern on the wooden deck, on our bare legs, on our hair and faces. Then she reaches over and gives me a hug and lies down and we lie there for ages, her hugging me (which is as weird as it sounds, yes) and swinging in the hammock and the rain plopping down harder and faster all around us, puddling on the deck, soaking through our clothes, trying to fill the lake up with all its hope and wetness.

18

It's right before dinner when everything goes wrong.

I'm at the counter, halfheartedly checking my email (nothing from Mars Now, nothing from Tig). Buzz Aldrin is squawking in his cage like he's trying to alert us to a fire. Iris is on the phone with her boyfriend in New York. And Elliott is lying on the couch, playing a loud video game on the Xbox. Every bullet and every crunching body sound hurts my head, almost as much as my empty inbox hurts my heart. I'm sleepy and cold and feel weird and wrong, like I'm on the cusp of something terrible, like I'm standing on the edge of a building, on a rooftop, wobbling in the wind.

I go, "Can you turn that down?"

"It's not loud," Elliott says, not looking up.

"Mom," I say, "It's too loud."

"Turn it down," Mom says, stirring the soup on the stove.

Rainy days are always soup days. She's making three-bean soup, which is usually my favorite, but today the smell of it sticks in the back of my throat and feels like a ball of wool, choking me. I'm so mad and sad, because I love that soup.

"No," says Elliott. "It's not even loud!"

I don't know how it happens, but next thing I know, I'm getting up and I have the whole bowl of apples in my hands and I'm dumping them on Elliott's head. There's a silence while we all watch the apples bounce one by one off her skull and onto the couch and the carpet, then she's up and she's so mad. I've never seen her so mad. And I know she's going to punch me. And I also sort of know that I deserve it, but that still doesn't make it less scary.

Then, in slow motion, she is flying over the back of the couch and trying to punch me and Dad comes running into the room and he's holding me back and laughing because he doesn't know what's going on and also because he's an inappropriate laugher. And I'm trying to push him off me and Iris is there, reaching over me to push Elliott away, and Mom is shouting, "STOP THAT RIGHT NOW!" and somehow Iris's hand gets tangled in my hair and then there's a funny tugging feeling on my scalp and then the room goes totally quiet and Iris is standing there, with my hair in her hand. Even Elliott's mouth drops open.

"Whoa," Elliott says. "Ish."

I just blink. *Tick, tick, tick.* I guess my mouth is open, too.

"Oh, Ish," Mom says, and then she's hugging me.

Iris is crying. She's just holding my hair in her hand,

but she's also trying to hug me with her empty arm and Dad has let go of me, and I feel like I'm falling.

"Don't touch me!" I say, whisper-quiet. "No one touch me!"

"I'm sorry!" Iris is shaking really hard now. "I'm sorry! I didn't know!"

Dad clears his throat. "We knew it might happen, I guess I just didn't know it could be this sudden," he says.

And I'm just standing there. I feel so embarrassed; I want to die. I want the floor to open up in a huge sinkhole. I want a meteor to crash through the ceiling. Something. Anything.

I don't know what to say or to do or even to think. My head feels weird and light and exposed and naked and my face is hot pink from blushing uncontrollably and I'm shaking, just like Iris was. I walk away from all of them and push open the sliding glass door. I have bare feet and the deck is hot under them, even soaking wet from the rain, even though it has stopped, leaving the air misty-damp, the sun drying the rain so fast that it's rising like smoke, in wafts.

I run across the deck quickly. I need to get away from them. From what happened. From my hair. My hair! My hands keep going to my scalp, searching and patting. The bare part of my scalp is as smooth and bald as a pool ball, like it doesn't even remember hair being there, like it had been waiting under there the whole time for the roots to let go.

It's not all gone. Just a huge chunk of it, a giant bald patch, like I'm a clown. My fingers rub the newly smooth skin spot. I picture Iris taking the handful of hair she's holding and putting it in the garbage can under the kitchen sink. I imagine her washing her hands for the length of the song on Dad's phone.

I'm not crying. I can't.

I hurry down the steps to the shore of the lake, and the cracked, hard beach feels a tiny bit cooler than it has, a little bit slimy, a lot wet.

I keep walking and walking. The lake level is so low, I can practically walk to the island. I walk out on the muddy, cracked ground until my feet are in the water and then I just keep going. I'm wearing jeans and they are the worst in water, but who cares? I'm waist deep and then I'm swimming. Swimming is harder than it used to be, I guess because of what I'm wearing and from all the throwing up. My jeans don't want to stay up. My arms don't seem to want to pull me through the water, but luckily, I touch down with my feet before I drown.

And then there I am, on Lunch Island.

Alone.

I've never been here without Tig, not even once.

I step carefully, like I might be disturbing someone. That's dumb, because of course there is no one here. I find our sign, "Mars 140 million miles." It's gone crooked, so I straighten it. Today, according to my calculator app,

Mars is actually 175,891,209 miles from Earth. Orbits! Think about it. Not that I'm going to change the sign, but it's still good to know. Maybe we should have left some of the digits blank and left a piece of chalk so we could change it. I take my Sharpie out of my pocket and write in tiny letters along the bottom "Distance Fluctuates Due To Orbits!" Which makes me feel better. I don't want to mislead anyone.

Then I'm hit with this weird, skin-crawling wave of embarrassment. Why did I come here? The wind is hot and it blows on the part of my skull that is naked. It will probably get sunburned and pink like one of those hairless baby rats. The main thing that I am thinking is that I can never go back to school now, not ever. I think about Kaitlyn's braids. She has so much hair! It isn't fair and it isn't fair and it isn't fair.

I sit down, but I don't lean against the sign so it doesn't fall over. It's not even pointing at Mars anymore, just to Oregon. Which is where Tig is right now, doing some normal non-sick-kid stuff, like eating a sandwich or playing Mars Defender on the Xbox.

When Gavriel was here, the emails that pinged in were from Tig. There were two of them.

The first one said:

Mom says you have a brain tumor!!!!!!!!! Is that true? Are you OK? Ish, it's gonna get better. It has to. I know it.

The second one said:

I'm going to come and see you. Wait for me.

I read the second one a bunch of times. *Wait for me.*
Like, what, I'm going to up and die before he can get
here from Portland? It's only a fifteen-hour drive!

Wait for me.

It's actually sort of old-fashioned and maybe even
romantic, but I don't want Tig to be romantic. I don't
want anything like that. I just want to be his BFF. I
want to build a fort on Lunch Island like we always said
that we'd do. I want to sleep here one night with him
and look at the stars and see who can find the most falling stars and who can find the most constellations and if
we can find Mars through the telescope. I want to make
a campfire and have s'mores.

Wait for me.

"I just want to go back to normal," I tell the sign. The
breeze blows my words smoothly into small diamond-
topped ripples on the lake. The leaves of the tree rustle
like they are agreeing with me, *yes, yes, yes, yes.* "Yes," I tell
them. "Exactly."

I gather up a bunch of rocks and start building a
fire pit that we can use when Tig comes. If he comes, I
mean. Maybe he was just saying that to be nice. The
rocks are heavy and I'm sweating. One rock at a time.
It feels kind of good, like it used to feel when I worked

out, my muscles trembling a bit from the effort, my lungs hurting from trying to breathe fast enough to keep up. I should do this all the time. I should do this every day so that I'm strong for Mars. I haven't been running around the lake. I haven't been doing anything. Maybe all the throwing up counts. My abs are as strong as steel.

I lift and place the rocks and lift and place the rocks until my arms are shaking and I have to stop. The thing with chemo is that it is the worst and also, it sucks all the energy out of me, leaving me as floppy as a piece of paper. I feel like I'm constantly carrying something heavy but that heavy thing is me. Now gravity is all wrong, there is too much of it. (Which there is, on Earth! On Mars, we'll actually be healthier. There will be less pressing down on us! Which, if you think about it, is what gravity is doing, squashing us like ants under a giant thumb.)

I lie back on the warm rock next to the future fire pit. I close my eyes, just for a minute. I can hear a bee buzzing, but I can't be bothered to worry about its stinging me. So what if it does? I have a brain tumor! My hair is falling out! A bee sting is nothing. The breeze feels slightly cool, which is nice. It smells like the lake always smells, like the hot, dry rock always smells, like Lunch Island always smells. I like it when things stay the same. I like that I can close my eyes and smell home. I guess I'll miss that on Mars.

If I get to go at all.

I'm starting to think that I won't. I squeeze my eyes shut even harder. "I'm still going!" I whisper to the rock, and the rock takes my words and makes them as true as fossils, seals them forever. "I'm going to be OK." I try to make it sound like I believe that.

I'm just starting to dream — I'm on Mars and I'm so relieved because I haven't dreamed of it for the last few times I've slept and I thought maybe it was gone, that I'd lost it — when I hear something splashing in the water. I can't be dreaming if there is splashing, because there's not enough water on Mars for splashing. It takes me a few seconds to figure out that it means that I'm awake, after all. I unglue my eyes, which is harder than it sounds, and I sit up. I'm dizzy. I wish I had water so that I could stop myself from throwing up. I dry heave a little bit, but nothing happens and it passes. I can see Iris coming through the water. She's not swimming, she's walking. I wave and she waves back. She's so pretty it makes me want to cry. She looks like a goddess or an angel or something too perfect to be real.

"Hey," Iris says, finally climbing up on the rock. "What are you doing?"

"Me?" I go. "Um, just sitting here. What are *you* doing?"

"This lake is a weird color," she says, almost like I haven't said anything. "I bet this water gave you that tumor. Mom and Dad should move. They should sue someone. It's not right."

I look at the water, which looks the same to me as

it always has, green and cool. I don't mention the perchlorate. It seems kind of beside the point now. Water bugs skim the surface. From this angle, you almost wouldn't know that the lake was shrinking, that it used to be huge and now it's just basically a pond.

"If it was the water, Tig would have a Brussels sprout, too," I point out. "I mean, a tumor."

Iris frowns. "Maybe," she says. "It's not fair."

"What isn't?" I say. "That I have Nirgal and he doesn't? He doesn't deserve it either! Why shouldn't it be me?"

"It just shouldn't!" she says. "You don't deserve it!"

"Neither does he!"

"But why you?"

"I don't know!" I shout.

"That stupid factory! They've basically killed you!" she shouts back. "Don't you get it? You're going to die! Why aren't you mad?"

"I am mad!" I shout. "I'm mad at YOU!"

I'm crying now. Why is she making me cry? She's supposed to make everyone happier! It's her job!

"I'm sorry," she goes, looking stricken. "I was just, I don't know what I was thinking, I shouldn't have said that. I'm sorry, Ish."

"Whatever," I say.

"I was thinking out loud. I shouldn't have said any of those things. You aren't dying."

"You're right, you shouldn't have. I *am* dying. I guess I am. No one wanted to say it, so I guess I should thank you for being the first person brave enough to put it into words. But I hate you. I unthank you. I wish you hadn't come home," I lie. I'm crying so hard that my words come out like tadpoles stuck in mud, bubbles in between each sentence. I choke-sob. She's crying, too. Pity party on Lunch Island, table for two!

"I didn't mean that last part," I say, hiccupping.

"I didn't mean that Tig should have a brain tumor," Iris says. "I just wish that you didn't. You call it Nirgal, huh?"

I shrug and roll my eyes. I wouldn't give my brain tumor to someone else, even if I could, but I wish it wasn't mine. Duh. Of course I wish that. "Don't ask me why I call it Nirgal, OK?"

"OK." She puts her hand on my leg. "I'm *so* sorry about your hair."

I nod. "Me, too!" I say. I try to slow my breathing back down to normal. I take her hand off my leg, gently. Then I wipe my eyes on my T-shirt, which is mostly dry now. "I knew it would fall out, I just thought it would happen slowly, not all at once like that."

"Yeah," she says. "It was like it just let go!"

I giggle. Her face when she saw my hair in her hand! I mean, it wasn't funny but it also sort of was.

"Are you crying again?" Iris asks.

"No," I say. I shake my head. Suddenly, I'm laughing really hard. "I always hated my dumb hair."

"What's funny?" Iris looks worried, but it's too late, I can't stop laughing. I think I'm going to pee my pants, that's how hard I'm laughing. A bunch of geese fly by, honking, like they are laughing, too, and finally she joins in a little at first, then a lot.

When we're done, we sit quietly without talking and watch the sun setting behind the hills. It's really pretty, but once the sun goes away the water turns black. It looks a little scary. It looks a little dangerous. Leeches, I think.

"Come on," Iris says. "I'll give you a piggyback ride back to the house."

I climb on. "Are you sure?" I ask, as she wobbles around unsteadily. "I'm heavy."

"No, you aren't," she says. "You don't weigh anything! You're like a feather."

"Am not," I say, but she's sort of right. I can see all my rib bones now, jutting up under my skin. My hips pop up like fists. Yesterday, I tried to ride my bike around the lake like I used to, but it's as if all my muscles just went away and left nothing holding up my bones. My calves are soft skin, nothing more. I don't know where all my toughness went. I only made it a block before I got sick and had to come home, wobbling the whole time. "I am not a machine," I murmur.

"Of course you aren't," Iris says. "Machines don't have hearts."

Iris wades through the water. I can feel the pull of it, the current she's making with each step. I want to let go and just float on my back, just float away, but I keep hanging on. By the time we get back, I'm shivering.

I go up to my room without saying anything to Mom or Dad or Elliott, who are sitting in the living room, watching a show, pretending to not be watching me. Yesterday, I saw Mom hugging Elliott and she didn't push her away. Maybe this brain tumor is good for something, after all.

I walk by Buzz Aldrin's cage. "Squawk," he goes. Then, "Houston, we have a problem."

"True fact," I tell him. His feathers are patchy and sparse. He's molting, just like me.

"Ish?" Mom calls.

"Come in and watch with us!" Dad says.

I don't answer or go in there because that way they don't have to talk to me. They don't have to think of what to say that isn't, "You're going to die." If it's true, then it must be what they are thinking all the time! Mom must be thinking about it while she works, spooning porridge into the old people's mouths, helping them walk down the hall, pushing their wheelchairs outside for fresh air. She must be thinking how it isn't fair that I'm not going to be an old person. Not ever.

I crawl into bed, and I start dreaming before I'm even all the way under the covers, that's how tired I am. That's how hard it is now, to even just stay awake, even when I'm so mad. Even when I'm so scared. Even when I want nothing more than to not be alone.

19

There's an emergency.

EMERGENCY EMERGENCY EMERGENCY

I know it's a dream, OK?

At least, I think it is.

I also know that my heart is racing: There is hardly any time. One minute, we are playing cards at the folding table, laughing, talking. The next minute, there's a huge cracking crash and the whole wall of the dome has caved in. Sand is blowing everywhere. The air tastes like rust. Trying to breathe is impossible, the air is as thin and oxygenless as death.

I'm struggling to get into my suit. *Help, help, help,* I'm thinking, but I can't say it because it's a waste of air and no one can help me. I don't know where Gav and Tig went. They were here! Playing cards! Maybe they were sucked out of here so quickly, they had no time to react.

The air is freezing cold and I'm shivering shivering shivering and I miss my mom and the soup she used to make when it rained. I frown. Why Mars? Why me?

But also, why not me? Someone had to be first. I remember thinking that. My memory is foggy. When

I was a kid, I had a brain tumor. Maybe that's the thing. The problem. Maybe it's back. I just can't think. It's frustrating. My head is colder than the rest of me, so I lift my hand up and touch my skull and it's as smooth as an egg, hairless. Bald.

The radiation on Mars would shrink that tumor to nothing, Tig was saying. When was he saying that?

I guess that's why I came. To shrink it. But I'm not a kid anymore. The suit is on now and my breathing is raspy against the ventilator.

I should have stayed on Earth. I should have had a Cinnabon and liked it and been happy when The Gap had a sale.

No, no. That's stupid. I like being here. I like being first. It's brave. I'm brave.

I list all the female astronauts I can think of: Valentina Tereshkova, Samantha Cristoforetti, Liu Yang, Yi So-yeon, Kalpana Chawla, Claudie Haigneré, Eileen Collins, Chiaki Mukai, Ellen Ochoa, Mae Jemison, Roberta Bondar, Helen Sharman, Sally Ride. They were all firsts. First at something. Then I add Mischa Love. First woman on Mars. Girl, I guess. First girl on Mars.

I have to be brave for this. For everyone else who will come after me. The protective panel has slammed down now. I am on the wrong side of it, so I'll have to walk through this storm to the door and go back in. Easy. I can do it. I take one step. The wind is pushing me back so hard, I feel squashed. But I keep going.

I have to be brave so that one day, someone will put my name on a list and memorize it. So I matter.

I look around and then I see him: Tig. "Tig!" I shout. My voice is strangled in my throat and I'm choking on dust, and then there he is and he's bald, too. Does he have a brain tumor? Was it the lake? It was our fault! We kept swimming when they said not to do it. He is coming toward me but he isn't in a suit and he's not going to make it. It's too late. I try to tell him but I can't, and the wind takes me and picks me up and slams me into a cliff wall. I'm on a cliff. I'm off a cliff. I'm falling. I've lost them all. I've lost everyone.

Brussels sprout, I remember, opening my eyes, trying to slow my breathing and calm down so that my throat can open, so that I can breathe. It's not real. It's just the Brussels sprout.

The house is still and dark and quiet. I get up out of bed. I'm still wearing wet jeans. I get changed into dry pyjamas. My skin is red and raw where the wet jeans were rubbing it. I must have been kicking in my sleep. I put the wet clothes in the hamper and make my bed. Being the only one awake in a still house is so lonely. I walk around from bedroom to bedroom and look inside. Elliott doesn't look tough when she's sleeping. Dad sleeps with his mouth wide open. What if a fly flew in? He snorts and rolls over. Iris just looks beautiful. I sit on the edge of her bed for a minute, but she doesn't wake up. She's probably dreaming about normal things.

Clothes and New York City and boys and happiness. Red, heart-shaped balloons.

I go downstairs into the kitchen and get a glass of water from Dad's reverse osmosis pitcher. I don't know if it tastes better than regular water, but it looks more interesting. I take tiny sips. The trouble with water is, it mostly tastes like whatever was last in your mouth. So, basically, it tastes like barf. Before chemo, I never knew it was possible to throw up this much! I would've thought you were lying if you said it was true. Now I know. My tongue wants to move out. It wants to go live in the mouth of someone who doesn't always taste like regret.

In the corner of the room, Buzz Aldrin is sleeping in his cage, with his feathers all puffed up. He looks almost cute. I walk over and look at him. He opens one eye and looks at me. "We have a problem," he says sadly. "Houston." Poor Buzz Aldrin. A clump of feathers is on the floor of his cage.

"I love you," I say to him. "We're both patchy."

I open the cage door and put my hand out. He looks super suspicious, like *What are you doing, Ish? It's the middle of the night!* "Come on," I tell him. "One small step for man, one giant leap for mankind! Or parrot-kind, I guess. Do it for all the other parrots, Buzz."

He hesitates and looks around his cage, like he's looking for someone to tell him it's OK.

"It's OK," I tell him. "Someone has to be first. Be brave."

Finally, he steps on to my finger. The weight of him is always surprising. He weighs as much as one of those rotisserie chickens that Mom buys when she's too tired to cook. Except he's alive, so the weight of him is different. It shifts and moves. I suddenly understand the phrase "dead weight."

Buzz Aldrin stretches out his wings and I can hear the *plit, plit, plit* sound of the feathers separating from each other. Then he pulls them in again.

"You'll see," I tell him. "Just wait till you see those stars. This will be worth it. Once in a lifetime type stuff, I promise."

I push open the sliding glass door as quietly as I can and I step out onto the deck. I bet he's never felt outside air before. That's what I'm doing for him: I'm giving him everything, everything, everything. "Smell it," I tell him. "Hold it in. See?" I take a deep breath and hold it in my lungs. I can imagine all my little lung fibers absorbing the oxygen. I can smell the trees and the water and the sky and the smell of the dry wood of the deck and the rubber of the hose coiled near my feet. Can parrots smell? I know that vultures can smell death from miles away. I don't want to think about that. I close my eyes and exhale it all again. "Isn't it great?" I ask him.

"Rabbit," Buzz Aldrin says, preening. I think he's nervous. He pulls each feather through his beak, looking at me from under his wing. "Rabbit," he says again.

The trees and the lake and the night are all my favorites. They are everything that I'll miss when I go to Mars. The night sky smells like that paint you use in kindergarten, the kind that you mix with water. Maybe it's the dew on the pavement, or just the wet night touching the dry day, but I love the smell of those paints. In kindergarten, Mrs. Poppe moved our seats around every month. One month, I sat next to Tig. It was the best month. We had one project where we had to paint this huge chicken. It was for Easter. I don't know what chickens had to do with Easter, to tell you the truth, but it didn't matter. We made that chicken into a rainbow. Rainbow Chicken. We worked on it all day. It was an amazing chicken. A miracle chicken. A chicken of God, I guess. Or Jesus, at least.

"I miss him," I tell Buzz Aldrin. "Tig, I mean. And the chicken." I carefully walk across the deck to the wooden chair and I sit down.

Buzz Aldrin's feathers are ruffling in the stirring air. He shifts his weight and I put him on my shoulder. Together, we watch the moon making a path over the water. The path basically leads from our deck steps right to Lunch Island. Lunch Island is almost exactly the same size and shape as Big Joe. Big Joe is a Martian Rock. When Tig and I named Lunch Island, we had a big fight. He wanted to call it Big Joe, but I said that name was already taken. I didn't want any Earth stuff to be the same as Mars stuff. I needed it to be different. All the best stuff had to be reserved for Mars.

Tig will go to Mars. He'll see Big Joe. He'll see that rock shaped like a crab. He'll go into the cave behind it and see what's in there. He'll find the Mars lady from the photos. Maybe she'll be me.

"It's not fair," I tell Buzz Aldrin, but I think he's gone to sleep again, nestled into my neck. The truth is that I've always been jealous of Tig because he's a boy and I'm not a boy. It would be easier to be a boy, I think. Boys just decide to do a thing and then they can do it. They don't have to be the first male anything, they just *do* stuff. There's a lot less pressure on them, if you think about it. A lot less gravity. All this time, both of us have been talking about going to Mars and when he says it, people say, "That's great! That's amazing!" And when I say it, they go, "Gosh, won't you be scared? Won't you miss everything?" And, worse, they don't believe me.

They always believe him. Because he's a boy.

It makes me hate him just a little bit, just like I hate Elliott a little bit for being so cute when she was a toddler, for being the one my parents picked, only to find that I was also coming along for the ride.

Maybe there's something wrong with me that I feel this way. Maybe that's why the Brussels sprout started to grow.

If I were a boy, I could just have a brain tumor and deal only with that. I wouldn't have to care that my hair was falling out. I wouldn't have to care that it would make me look like a boy because I'd already be a boy.

I start to cry, and Buzz Aldrin wakes up and squawks.

"Shh," I tell him. "You're just a bird. You don't understand."

Buzz Aldrin stares at me.

"I'm going to die," I explain to him.

Iris said it, so it must be true.

They must know it's true.

Someone, somewhere said it was, and now it is.

When I first got diagnosed, I asked the doctor if I was going to die. He had a long beard and crooked teeth. His hair was tied up in a bun. He blinked at me, silently, like a snake. There was no *tick tick*. Then he said, "Not if I can help it!" in this upbeat way that doctors have when they talk to kids.

Now, replaying it in my head, I run it through my mental decoder and I hear what he was really saying, which was "Yes."

"I don't want to die," I tell Buzz Aldrin and he squawks again, like he's agreeing with me. "I'm not done here yet! Plus, I'm scared." For a second, we stare into each other's eyes, mine blue and his pink. In between us, there's purple. "Do you see it?" I say to him. He winks. I'm sure, he winks. "The thing with dying," I say to him, "is that you have to do it alone. No one goes with you. You're all by yourself."

He squawks. Once, twice. Then suddenly he spreads

his wings. He squawks again, like he can't believe this, and then before I can do anything to stop him, he's flapping hard.

Then he's flying away.

He's soaring up there — he's way faster than I would have thought he could be — getting smaller and smaller, just a white splotch in the sky, smaller than the moon but bigger than the stars.

"Buzz Aldrin!" I call, but I know he's not coming back. He's never coming back.

My hand is shaking like crazy. What have I done? I let Buzz Aldrin go! I miss him so bad and so instantly, my stomach hurts, but it isn't my stomach, it's my heart, it's everything.

I bend double, thinking that I'm going to throw up, but I don't. I just sit like that for a while, looking at the light starting to spill onto the boards of the deck, the light from the rising sun making puddles of gold around my feet, bathing them in all this warm goldness that feels like it's sinking into me and making me sleepy again. The sun is so pretty when it rises. I'll miss this: the golden light of Earth. The latest pictures from Mars say that the light there is more green than gold. I don't know how I feel about that.

I sit up. Then I go inside. I pour the last of the cereal into a big bowl and dump all of the milk on it. Then I take it outside and I start to eat. I eat and eat and eat until I feel more full than I ever have. Then I go to the hammock and climb in. The sun is like a blanket that covers me entirely. I fall asleep so deeply that this time, I don't even dream at all, swinging back and forth in all that perfect, warm Earth-morning light.

20

"If you want, I can cut it really short for you," says Iris. I'm sitting in front of the bathroom mirror, brushing my hair. It's not all coming out, but lots of it is. It's weird, but I can't stop doing it. I mean, I don't want to be bald, but it's sort of like poking a bruise. It's a bad feeling that's also good. Or not good, but compelling. I couldn't stop if I wanted to! The brush pulls gently and my scalp sighs and releases. The sink is full of long red hair. It's hard to believe there is any still on my head, but there is. Lots of it.

"Shave it," I say, trying to sound brave. I always used to hate my ugly red hair. Now I don't, but it's too late. That's life, I guess. When I'm bald, I'll look like cancer kid. But I am cancer kid. So.

This afternoon, I have to go in for another treatment of chemo. Chemo that feels like metal is being poured into me, drop by drop by drop. I'm like the lake, only I'm being polluted on purpose. All the rainbow trout will die. Only the goldfish will be left, swimming around in a sad circle, wondering where everyone went. The goldfish is the smallest piece of me, but also the most important, I guess. I don't know what I mean by that. The Brussels sprout is growing longer tendrils that are curling around all the things that used to make sense to me.

"OK," Iris says. She's stroking my hair. Even as she does that, it's slipping out and onto the floor, like tiny invisible hands are releasing it. I shiver. "Want me to do it?"

"Leave me alone," I say, which is the opposite of what I mean.

Iris gasps and steps back. "I'm sorry," she goes.

"Whatever," the me-that-is-not-me says as she leaves the room. "WHATEVER, OK?"

This kind of thing is starting to happen. It isn't me! I want to explain. There are tendrils!

This morning, I (or a tendril!) sent Tig an email that said:

Don't be stupid, you don't have to come here. You don't have to pretend we are still friends just because you feel bad for me that I have cancer. You don't have to say you love me. Go away.

Love, Ish.

After I sent it, I was super embarrassed. Who signs a "GO AWAY" note with "Love, Ish"? Only me. Dumb.

But maybe it wasn't me! Maybe it was the tendrils! Maybe the Brussels sprout is becoming the command center. Maybe I'm not in charge anymore.

I shake my head at my reflection. "Rude," I tell it. "There's no excuse."

One of my doctors says that in order to fight it, I've got to think of the Brussels sprout as cancer instead of as a Brussels sprout. "Think real thoughts," he says. "This is a real war you're fighting."

I think he's dumb. He's never even had a Brussels sprout! What does he know? It doesn't really matter what I think of it. It's not a war. I can't do anything about it. It's still there, no matter whether I call it Nirgal or cancer or a Brussels sprout. It's still growing. It's taking over. Now I'm scared that it's bigger than everything that I used to be. I'm a (dying) star; it's a galaxy. Or maybe it's a black hole that is pulling me in and I'm imploding into elements, but in slow motion, so slow that no one knows it is happening but me.

I keep brushing and my hair keeps falling and I'm staring at myself in the mirror like I'm a show that I'm watching on TV. Brush, brush, fall, fall. Bald patches are shining through all over, like stars filling up the night sky.

Not everything is about the stars, I tell myself. *You're so boring with all this celestial stuff. You aren't a star, it's not a black hole, and you're annoying.* It's pretty interesting how it's not even at all hard to hurt your own feelings if you try. I put the brush down and sit down on the floor. The tiles are bluish white and have a gray pattern that runs through them that reminds me of veins. Or tendrils. Or I don't know what. I trace them with my pointer finger. The tiles are cool and solid. It makes me feel better, tracing those lines that go nowhere, ignoring the long strands of my red hair that block my path.

"OK," says Iris, coming back into the room. Her eyes are pink, like she's been crying. "I'm going to leave you alone. But call me if you need me."

I shrug, like I don't care, when really I do. *Come back!* I want to say but don't.

I stand up and get back to brushing, staring at my own face. My eyes are really bright blue, like lakes. I blink my lakes. *Slish, slosh, slish, slosh.* I look into the center of my eyes for islands. Maybe a tree. Mars: 140 million miles (sometimes). I'm dizzy. My head feels thick. The sprout is in the gravy. Once we had a big earthquake and the lake shifted back and forth and the water rose and fell like when you purposely make waves in a bathtub. You could see it. I don't know what made me think of that.

I hear Iris walking away down the hallway and then hesitating before going down the stairs. I close the door and lock it but then Elliott is banging on it. "Let me in! I have to pee before school!"

I grin. If she treats me normally, I feel more normal. Make sense? It's like the more people (Iris) treat me like I'm going to break, the more I feel like I probably am.

"Go away," I yell back.

"MOM," she yells. "CAN I USE YOUR BATH-ROOM? ISH HAS LOCKED HERSELF IN. AGAIN."

I brush with longer and longer strokes that pull more and more hair out, pressing harder and harder, until my scalp stings like a million tiny bee stings. "Stop," I tell myself, but I keep going.

I put the brush down on the counter and use some toilet tissue to wipe the hair out of the sink. There is so much of it. Handfuls and handfuls. I put it in the garbage. My hair is still long, except for the bald patches, but it's thin. It looks like the old people's hair at Mom's work. You can see all that scalp shining through. It really does shine. Why are scalps so shiny? There's probably some reason that sounds like the punch line to a joke, but I can't think of it. The only joke I can think of is this one: Q: What do you call a cow during an earthquake? A: Milkshake!

Is that funny? I smile at myself in the mirror. I laugh. It looks weird. I look weird.

Mom knocks on the door. "It's time to go!" she says, in her fake-bright voice.

"OK, OK, OK," I say, in a madder voice than I mean to use. "I'm *coming*."

I grab some of my Mars books from my room and I follow her down the stairs. I don't want her to look at me. I don't want her to see the truth about my cancer shining all over my skull. *Look at me!* it screams. *I'm shining!*

I walk past Buzz Aldrin's empty cage. It makes my stomach feel funny. I wonder where he ended up. I wonder if he died. I wonder if he minded that at all. I also wonder why no one has cleaned his cage and put it away in the basement. It's still dirty with parrot drop-pings. His food bowl is still half-full. He wasn't finished! Not one person in my family got mad at me for letting him go. That's pretty weird, if you think about it. He wasn't just mine, he was part of the family. He belonged to all of us. Weren't they mad? I guess no one can tell me they're upset with me anymore. I guess they wouldn't feel right doing that now that I'm sick and as breakable as glass. I run my hand along the cage bars, and it makes a sound like music.

"We're late!" Mom calls back to me.

I can hear her trying to be patient. I can hear her working really hard at not doing any regular Mom-yelling, any "GET OUT HERE RIGHT NOW."

"Coming, Mom," I singsong.

It's still hot outside. We open the car doors and a wave of hot air comes flowing out, like it's been trapped (which it has, if you know anything about the green-house effect). In order to really live on Mars, we'll have to re-create the greenhouse effect. It shouldn't be hard. Humans seem super good at that.

Dad zooms by on his bike. "Good luck today!" he shouts, and then he's off.

We get into the car and slam the doors. I watch Dad pedaling. His legs are so strong that he's up the hill before we are, his bike tip-topping side to side from the effort. I close my eyes and pretend that I'm him, that I'm strong, feeling the hot air rushing by my face, feeling my heart speed up to carry me farther and faster, gulping down all that cold clear water from the always present water bottle clipped to the bike's frame like it's my full-time job. Instead, I'm in a hot car, my weak body barely wanting to sit upright. I crank up the air conditioner, which blows even hotter air at our faces before cooling off the tiniest bit. I groan. The hot air makes me feel like throwing up.

Everything makes me feel like throwing up.

Iris is in the backseat. The plan is that she is going to hang out with me at chemo because Mom has to work. She's taken off too much time already, they've said. She can't use it all at once. The old people need her. Besides, she might need more time later. (That means "when I get sicker" if you read between the lines, which I try not to do.) I don't appreciate their pessimism but I can see where they're coming from. I mean, I guess if I die, she'll need a whole bunch of time to cry and to remember how I was.

What will she say at my funeral? "All Ish wanted to do was not be on Earth." Well, I guess if it's my funeral, then I must have got my wish, after all. If I'm dead, I won't be on Earth anymore, if you think about it that way.

I blink back some tears. Do not cry, I tell myself firmly. I'm a machine, OK?

"What?" says Iris. "Did you just say that you're a machine?"

"No," I go. "Why would I say that? Lame."

"Sorry," she says.

I want to tell her that it's OK. It's not her, it's me! I don't know what's wrong with me! Except I do know what's wrong with me. What's wrong with me is cancer. There, I said it. Now it can go away.

I squish my eyes shut tightly and will it away. *Go away cancer go away cancer go away cancer go away cancer you are cancer not a Brussels sprout so now you can go away.*

Nothing happens. I open my eyes. We pass the ice cream shop, which is still shut, only someone has smashed the front window so it looks like a face, the mouth wide open in an *O*.

"Are you sure you know where to go?" Iris looks nervous.

"It's not hidden. It's on Four North. There are signs. You can't get lost. And it's no big deal," I tell her. "It's just a row of chairs and a bunch of people getting medicine and playing Xbox. It's sort of like being at a bad party. The worst party."

"OK," she says. "I'm just nervous." Poor Iris. She should be in New York! She should be winning her competition! Her weird clothes that she makes are crazy beautiful, even if they don't have anything to do with Mars. I don't say it to her or anything, but it's totally a stretch to call it "Mars fashion." On Mars, "fashion" is going to be space suits. Practical things. It's like un-fashion. She's made Mars into the worst of what Earth has to offer. All sparkly and shiny and too much.

Like in her Mars world, everything has feathers: white ones, iridescent ones.

"I found them at the flea market," Iris told me. "Boxes and boxes of them. It was like magic, finding those. Like you'd never think that you could say to yourself, I need some iridescent feathers! and then walk out of your apartment and find someone selling ten boxes of exactly what you want." I nodded, but what I was thinking was that of course that would happen to Iris, of course there were ten boxes of shiny feathers exactly when and where she needed them. Iris would never grow a vegetable in her brain. It wouldn't occur to the vegetable to grow there, period. Iris would only go to Mars if it was shiny and feathery and silly. I hate her for making Mars silly.

I snap my seat back, fast, right into her, bashing her knees.

"Hey!" Iris says, now. "Ouch."

"Sorry," I say. "The lever-thingy slipped." But that isn't true, not even a bit.

I don't know who I'm turning into. Someone who isn't any good. Maybe if I'm awful enough, though, they won't be sad when I die. If I die.

Maybe they wouldn't be anyway.

Who is going to miss me? I know Mom and Dad will. But Elliott won't. Tig won't. The kids at school won't. I'll just be the dead cancer kid, I won't be who I was waiting to become: I was going to be someone important! I was going to matter!

But they won't know that. They'll just remember that I was never really friends with them and I was kind of mean.

Great.

Mom drops us at the front door and I drag myself out into a wave of hot air. The heat wobbling on the pavement makes me feel dizzy, like I might faint. I lean on Iris so I don't fall. The hospital air conditioning is a welcome relief.

Iris makes chitchat all the way up. "Oh, the view is so pretty!" "Wow, what a nice room!" "Whoa! Look at that vending machine!" I give her a look and we both giggle. It's true that the vending machine is pretty impressive. It takes up the whole wall of one hallway. You can buy anything in there. You can even buy socks. They are four dollars, in case you are curious. I've never seen anyone buy them, but suddenly I really want them. I didn't bring any money, though.

I get my favorite chair, which is good. It's at the end of the row, so you can look out over the town through the window. It's still warm from when the last kid was sitting here. I wonder who it was. I wonder if he/she has cancer in their brain or somewhere else. I wonder if he/she has a better cancer.

Through the window, I can see the school. I guess the cafeteria is finished being painted, because even when I'm here at lunchtime, I don't see kids outside anymore. I feel an ache in my chest because I hate that dumb school but I'd do anything to be there again, hating it, watching the hands drag around on the clock while Mr. Wall teaches something pointless to a bunch of sweating, bored seventh graders. I never did find out what happened to the coyote! I want to know!

"Want to play Xbox?" says Iris.

She looks hopeful, so I say yes even though video games make my head hurt more than ever because of all that movement and noise and flashing. She starts it up and the Brussels sprout pulses like the light on the side of my laptop, like breathing.

The technician comes over and smiles at me. "Can't stay away, can you, Ish?" he says. He reaches into his pocket. "Pick a color," he says.

"Um, brown," I say, to try to make it impossible.

He reaches in and pulls out a brown lollipop.

"How did you know I'd say that?"

"I'm psychic," he says, winking.

I put the sucker into my mouth. Root beer. I love root beer, but it makes my stomach lurch. I take it out and put it back in its wrapper. "I'll have it after," I say. "Thanks."

He pats my shoulder. "See you in a couple of hours."

He hooks me up to the tubes and the hot metal taste floods my mouth. The medicine pours all through me like I'm a sieve, and it just flows through everything: bone, muscle, organs, hair. My eyes feel soft, like they're melting. It's such a sad, terrible feeling and I want to cry, but we're playing a racing game so I can't even blink or

I'll be off the track, spinning out of control. We play for an hour before Iris goes, "You look sleepy! Have a nap, I'll just do some drawings!"

"I'm not," I say, but I put the controller down. Right away, the freckled kid's mom grabs it, like she's been waiting for us to stop hogging it. I stick out my tongue, but she doesn't see it. If she had seen me, I would have explained about how that's "Hi!" in Tibet. The freckled kid is the worst. He drives everyone crazy. He's so hyper that they have to strap him to the seat or else he ends up jumping up when something exciting happens in his game. He's pulled his IV out about twenty times since this whole dumb thing started. I shoot him a sympathetic look, but he's not looking at me, he's already firing up Minecraft. At least when he's playing Minecraft, he's calm. He gets quiet.

I sit for a while in a half-sleep, half-not-sleep state and watch Iris draw. My head is itchy, but I'm scared that if I scratch it, the rest of my hair will come out. If that happens here, I'll die. I'll have to ask someone to throw it away for me. I wonder if somewhere in the back, there is a garbage can where they put all our hair. I'll shave it off later. It's better to let it go when I want to, not when it decides to do it by itself.

I really want ice cream. I open my mouth to ask Iris, but it's like my voice is part of the half of me that's sleeping. Maybe when we leave I can get Iris to stop for ice cream with me, but I guess there isn't anywhere to get it. I forgot for a second that the ice cream place is closed. My feet are cold, so I reach down and rub them, but that makes them itchy, so I stop. I am so tired that I nearly fall asleep like that, bent over, scratching my foot.

I'm still curved down like that when I hear a big ruckus in the hallway. I look up. Even Freckles puts down his Minecraft remote. Is it an earthquake? My heart starts beating harder. Then the door swings open and Mr. Wall comes through. He has the entire class with him and they are all staring at me.

I blink. Then blink again. *Tick, tick, tick.* My eyes are as dry and soft as marshmallows.

Am I asleep? I honestly can't tell. The kids are all wearing masks. Visitors have to. Those dumb paper masks protect us from all their germs, although I don't know how. What germ in its right mind can't figure out how to just go out the side?

I nod to Freckles, a nod that is meant to transmit "They are with me! I'm sorry but also not sorry because I'm kind of impressed that this many people want to visit me! Go back to your game!" I hope none of their germs sneak out the side gaps and kill Freckles, but I can't help smiling, even though I'm worried.

Then suddenly they are all singing. They're singing "Happy Birthday." I forgot it was my birthday! Who forgets their own birthday? There are Mom and Dad and even Elliott. She's carrying a balloon, which is red. On the balloon, she has written "THE RED PLANET

WISHES YOU A HAPPY BIRTHDAY." Then I'm crying because I forgot it was my birthday and because Elliott is being nice to me and all these people seem to like me even though I've always had secret mean thoughts about them and because I have cancer and the chemo is turning my veins into melted metal and because I'm so tired and because because because reasons.

I'm thirteen! Thirteen.

I'm a teenager!

I don't feel any different except for all the ways in which I do feel different, mostly to do with the Brussels sprout. I'm crying so hard now that I'm doing that hitching-breath thing that little kids do when they can't stop crying, but I'm not even that embarrassed. Maybe a little bit.

They finish singing and then they all clap for some reason, then everyone is clapping, except that one kid who is asleep. I feel this weird feeling, this heavy rush of love for every single person in the room.

I guess I love you, Tig said. But then he never came. I told him not to and he didn't. That's not love.

I cry a little bit more because my hair is falling out and they're all staring at me and pretending not to and I love them but I can't tell them that and then they are passing me cards and the weird metal hot taste in my mouth from the chemo is leaking out of me like a cloud. I hope they can't smell it.

They only stay for a few minutes, and then they are

gone again, all of them, just me and Iris and the freckled kid and his mom and the cake and the other kid who is asleep still, like nothing happened.

"That was weird, wasn't it?" I go to Iris, and she shakes her head.

"No, Ish," she says. "It was really nice."

I frown. I feel confused. But mostly I feel sleepy.

"When I fall asleep, I dream that I'm on Mars," I tell her. "Well, sometimes. Not every time. But I try to." I can't explain to her what I mean, which is that more and more, lately, I've been having regular dreams. Dreams where I try to make a phone call to call for help but I can't press the buttons. Dreams where I'm on Lunch Island and waves come up and I'm trapped. Dreams where I'm at school and there's a test and I didn't study. Normal-person dreams. I want to have the Mars dreams so bad, but they only come when they want to come, and they are different. They really are. Like in a regular dream, you can be walking with a dog on a leash and suddenly the dog isn't a dog anymore, it's a tiger or something, and you take that in stride because it's a dream, and you can walk on water and fly and do anything. My Mars dreams don't have tigers. "Don't have tigers," I manage to get out.

Iris smiles at me. "Are you falling asleep? What about the tigers?"

Her teeth are big and white and even, like they've been carved from those white stones you find at the beach sometimes and make wishes on. The real beach. The ocean beach. Not the lake beach, which isn't really a beach at all.

"That's great, Ish. I know you love Mars. Tell me what you dream about."

"Um." I wish I hadn't started. I can't make the words come out. "Tired," I say, instead of saying what I mean, about the biomes and the storm and *The Velveteen Rabbit*. When I say it like that, it does sound like a tiger on a leash, after all, and then without realizing it, I'm under, I'm asleep, I'm dreaming. I dream about school. I dream that I go back and there's a test but I haven't studied and I've wet my pants and everyone is laughing and laughing and hugging me, like I'm in on the joke, and in the dream, I try, I really do. I laugh with them and they pat my smooth head and I'm wearing a sparkly green cardigan that would look great with my hair if I had any and Kaitlyn is saying, "So cuuuuute," and I'm smiling and agreeing and all around us, everyone is laughing like a donkey. And it's not so bad, for a dream. It's kind of nice. It's easier than Mars. It's easier just being in that dream and having it all happening to me than always having to be the one who has to work really hard, the one who has to be there for everyone, the one who has to save the day.

21

Fish-boy turns up the next day, just when I thought he'd stopped caring about me at all. He wasn't at the birthday sing-along. I don't know where he was. He comes right into my bedroom, like he doesn't even have to knock. I was sleeping! Well, not really, but a bit.

"Hey," he says. "Happy late birthday and stuff."

"Gavriel," I say. "You don't have to keep coming over. It's weird. We don't even know each other! I'm not interested in being the cancer-kid-who-you-feel-sorry-for. No, thanks."

"What?" he says. "We know each other plenty. You're Ish and I'm Gav. It's not my fault you have cancer. I'm not going to unknow you."

I frown. "We weren't friends before I had cancer. I didn't even know you!"

"We would probably have been friends," he says.

"Not," I say.

"Would so," he says.

"Would not," I say. "I'm not really a 'friends' person."

He laughs. "What?"

I shrug. "I only have one friend."

"Yeah?" he says. "That's weird."

"Is not," I say.

"Is so," he says, grinning.

"Look," I say. "I get that this is something your mom is making you do. I'm just saying you don't have to. Or if you do have to, you can just sit there or watch a movie on the iPad or something. We don't have to talk." I blink a few times. My headache is one of those things that grows and shrinks. Gavriel is making it grow. "Anyway," I add. "We wouldn't have been friends. You called me Fish!"

"I was nervous!" he says. "It was my first day at a new school!"

"Are you crazy?" I say. "It was everyone's first day at a new school!"

"I didn't know anyone!"

"I give up," I say. "You're giving me a headache."

"You have a brain tumor!" he says. "I think it's probably the brain tumor that is giving you a headache."

He has a point, so I shrug.

"Ha!" he says. "You know I'm right. You don't like other people to be right, do you?"

"Of course, I do," I say as frostily as I can.

"OK," he says. "What if I say that no one can ever live on Mars because even if they solve the perchlorate problem, there's so much radiation that everyone would die?"

"You know about the perchlorate problem?" I go, kind of amazed. I mean, the perchlorate problem doesn't get as much press as it should.

"And," he says. "That moon, Phobos, they think it might break into lots of pieces and make a ring, but there's also a chance it will just slam into the planet and obliterate everything."

I look at him suspiciously. "Have you been reading about Mars to impress me?"

"Maybe." Gav grins. "I don't know. I actually didn't mean to. I just started and it was interesting so I kept reading." He shrugs. "I probably have a lot of it wrong."

"Probably," I echo, even though he really doesn't. He's pretty much exactly right. The radiation would kill everyone. Of course, I get radiated every day, but I guess that's different. Well, it isn't really different. It might kill me, too. It's funny how you spend your whole life avoiding something — no X-rays, they are dangerous! don't stand too close to the microwave! don't put your iPhone under your pillow! — and then, all of a sudden, to save your life, you're practically microwaving your whole head in desperation. I think about saying all that to Gavriel, not because he'll understand, but because he's here, but I don't bother because talking that much seems like it would be tiring.

Gavriel spins on the desk chair (which is annoying), practically knocking over a whole pile of books. "Oops," he says. "Want to go for a walk around the lake? This is boring."

"No," I go, right away, without thinking about it. "I'm sick, idiot. Sorry to be so dull."

"You're not dead," he says. "Your mom says we should get outside for fresh air or whatever."

"She didn't," I say.

"Yeah, she did," he says. "Your dad said, 'Take water!'" He holds up two water bottles. "See?"

"Oh," I say.

The truth is that I haven't gone for a walk for a long time. I used to run all the way around the lake at least four times a week! Going for a walk seems like a sad, old-person alternative to that. I am more like a sad old-person than I am like old-me, the me of last year, who (if things were completely different) would right now probably be running on that familiar path, my feet slip-slapping the dirt in the way they always had, while I counted the number of steps I took between breaths.

Then, out of nowhere, the Brussels sprout hands me this thought: "Fish-boy is sort of cute."

"No!" I say out loud. "He is *not*."

"Are you OK?" he says, looking scared.

"I'm fine," I go. "Look, why do you like me? Why are you doing this?" I don't mean to ask that, it just comes out, like the Brussels sprout is sitting on my filter and I can't stop myself from blurting. The Brussels sprout is a terrible ship's captain, I can tell you that. If I were a spaceship, it would have just steered me directly into a falling meteor. Boom. Then we'd all be dead.

There's a silence long enough that I die inside.

I'm dead.

The end.

Just kidding! But it's a long silence.

"Who said I liked you?" Gav goes. Then he laughs. Then he stops and stares at me. Then he goes, "I guess I do kind of like you. You're different from other girls. Anyway, I've always liked girls better than boys. Mostly. Before we moved here, my best friend was a girl. I guess I just … um, relate to girls more?"

"Yeah?" I say. I try to think if I know anything about Fish-boy, but I don't. "How?"

He shrugs. "Do you ever feel like maybe you made a mistake? Like just before you were born, you were meant to choose 'girl' and you chose 'boy' instead?" He blushes and takes a deep breath, like he's about to tell me something really scary or personal or both. He clears his throat. "Um, when I was littler, I used to wear dresses."

"Oh," I say. Then unexpectedly, even though I know it's the wrong reaction, I laugh, like it's really funny. *Hee-haw, hee-haw, hee-haw*. I'm practically channeling Kaitlyn. That's not even my laugh! It isn't even funny!

He looks mad or sad. Both, I guess. "I wouldn't have told you if I thought you'd laugh. I kind of don't know why I told you. We aren't good enough friends for me to blab all my feelings out! Uh," he pushes his hand through his hair. "This is awkward. I'm, like, embarrassed." He squints at me, like he's actually mad. "I thought you'd get it."

"That's not fair," I say, quietly. "I was just caught off-guard! I didn't have time to think about it!" I lie very still. The sunlight plays with the curtain and throws a shadow on the ceiling that looks like a wing.

Gavriel spins the chair around faster and harder.

"Look," I say. "I get it, OK? I used to think I should have been a boy because then everything would be easier. People would take me seriously and stuff like that. But then I realized I don't want to be a boy. I like being a girl. I guess I wish people didn't treat girls so crappily all the time, assuming we care about our hair more than we care about the perchlorate problem."

"Huh," he says. He stops spinning. "I don't think that's the same, though."

"Maybe not," I concede.

"So you don't want to go for a walk?" he goes, standing up really fast. "If you don't, I gotta go do something."

"I do! I want to," I say. "I will. I just have to do something first. Do you want to help me?"

"I guess," he says. "Is it something gross?"

I shake my head and point at the bathroom door. "Come on," I say.

We go into the bathroom. I can tell he's really embarrassed. He probably doesn't go to the bathroom with a lot of girls. That's when I notice that his T-shirt has a My Little Pony on it. Maybe he wasn't lying. Maybe he is a girl on the inside. I make a point of not looking at it, though, so I don't embarrass him.

I open the drawer and I take out Mom's hair-cutting scissors. I can't believe I'm doing this. It's like my body is being operated by someone else. Maybe Nirgal has taken over completely now. "I am not myself," I whisper. I hand the scissors to Fish-boy.

"What?" he says.

"Nothing," I go. He's not Tig! the voice in my head reminds me. Don't get confused! I hesitate. It's true that if Tig were here, I would totally have asked him to do this. But he isn't here. Gavriel is like Tig lite. Actually, he's nothing like Tig. My hand wobbles. I put the scissors down on the sink. Then I pick them up again.

"Cut," I say, handing them to him.

"No way," he says. "Um, you want me to cut your hair?" He looks super unhappy. "Why?"

"No, my nose," I go. "Of course, my hair."

"I don't know how to cut hair!"

"Please," I say. "It's all falling out. I'm going to shave it off, but first you have to cut it really short."

He snorts his breath in like he's going to choke. "I can't," he says.

"Then give them to me, I'll do it," I tell him. I grab the scissors from his hand and I start chopping. It's harder than it sounds. Those things only cut through small bits at a time, not big chunks! I saw off a big chunk of hair and it falls onto the floor. We both stare at it. He looks up and his eyes meet mine. His eyes are nice, big and brown. They look soft, like puppies. Actually, they are kind of girly, come to think of it. Mom told me once that sometimes people are born into the wrong bodies. Maybe he's one of those people. Maybe it makes sense.

Maybe, in a weird way, Gavriel is my first real girl friend. Except he isn't a girl.

"OK," he says. He steels himself with a big breath, which he lets out slowly. "I'll do it." He takes the scissors from my hand and starts cutting. I close my eyes. It feels nice, the sound of the scissors on my hair, the weight of it tumbling to the floor. My head gets lighter and lighter. I think about birds. I think about Buzz Aldrin and how he lifted off. My hair is lifting off.

It takes a pretty long time. And then, he's done. "OK," he whispers, like he's scared. "I'm done."

I open my eyes. All over my head — except for the bald patches — my hair is sticking up in short tufts. "I look like a hedgehog!"

"It's not that bad!" he says. Then he laughs. "You sort of do."

"I know," I go. "It's OK."

Then I get out Dad's shaving stuff.

"I don't know how to do this part," he goes. "I can't. What if I cut you?"

"How hard can it be?"

"I don't know! But maybe you should ask your dad to help." He looks scared. The razor is one of those old-fashioned ones. It looks sharp and dangerous. We both stare at it on the counter.

"OK," I say. "You go get him."

"OK," he says. I hear him going down the stairs. I rest my face against the cold tile on the wall. I like how it feels. Solid. Permanent. The tile doesn't have a brain tumor. The tile isn't going to die. The tile won't go anywhere. I wonder if there will be tile on Mars. *You'll never know*, the voice in my head tells me. *You won't be there. You won't get to go now. Not ever.*

"Shut up," I say out loud.

The door swings open.

"Dad's not home," Elliott goes. "But I'll do it. I've got this." She grabs the razor. It glints in the light like tiny diamonds reflecting off water.

I blink. *Tick, tick, tick.* Fish-boy is standing behind her, raising his eyebrows, like "Is this OK?" And I'm signaling him with my eyes, "No! This isn't OK!" But Elliott already has a lather going in Dad's fancy shaving bowl and then she's smoothing it all over my hedgehog bristly scalp with this big brush and it feels so nice that I forget to tell her to stop.

"How do you know how to do this?" I say.

"I used to watch Dad when I was really little," Elliott says. She shrugs. "I don't remember why."

"This dad?" I say. "I mean, our dad? I mean …"

"Yes." The razor swoops swoops swoops over my skull. "I don't remember our other dad."

"You have two dads?" says Gavriel, looking confused.

"We were adopted," I explain.

"Oh," he goes. "But you're really sisters?"

I shrug.

Elliott goes, "We're really sisters anyway, idiot."

"Yeah," I echo.

"Sorry," he says. He looks embarrassed.

"It's OK," I tell him. "Don't worry."

Elliott laughs. "Everyone's family is mixed up, right? Yours probably is, too." She shoots him a look.

"Yeah," he goes. "I mean, I guess. I don't have a dad. Well, he died."

"Sorry," Elliott says. She does look really sorry. Her hand wobbles a bit and the razor nicks my scalp.

"Hey!" I go. "You can't concentrate when you're talking."

"Yeah, yeah, sorry, Little Sister," she goes.

A lump forms in my throat and my eyes just about overflow. "Little Sister." I don't know why that makes me want to cry! Why isn't Elliott being mean to me? I'm so dizzy, but I don't want her to stop, so I balance myself by holding the edge of the sink.

"Are you OK?" Elliott says.

I nod.

"Don't nod!" she says. "I'll cut your head."

I nod again. "Seriously," she says. "Stop." She sticks her tongue out a little bit, which she's always done when she's concentrating. She's working on the area around my ears. I look so weird! I look terrible. My forehead looks enormous. I want to sob out loud, but instead I try to distract myself by thinking about the names of all the Mars missions that have ever taken place: Mariner, Viking, Kosmos, Spirit, Curiosity. My mind goes blank. I can't remember. I can't remember! I close my eyes. I remind myself to calm down. I'm a machine, I say to Nirgal, the Brussels sprout of planets.

"No, you're not," it answers. "You're the Earth."

"Can't I at least be Mars?" I ask.

"No," it says. "You are what you are." Then it adds, "Anyway, Mars is doomed."

"So's Earth," I tell it.

"Exactly," it says.

"Are you talking to me?" says Elliott.

"No!" I say. "I'm not talking."

Elliott and Gavriel look at each other. "Okaaaayyy," they say at the same time. "What?" I say, defensively. "Maybe I was just thinking out loud."

Elliott steps back and examines my head from all angles. She carefully puts the blade down on a towel and wipes it. "I'm done," she says.

We all stare at me in the mirror. I look like I'm wearing a Halloween costume! My head is as lumpy as Deimos. I don't know what to do with my face. I don't know how to arrange my mouth and eyes so that I don't look as scared as I feel.

"Thanks," I manage to say. "Now let's go for a walk."

"Don't you mean, 'Thank you Elliott, you're the best!'?" she says.

"Oh," I say. "I guess. I mean, thanks. Big Sister."

"Anytime, Ish," she says, grinning.

I wait for her to say something mean, but she doesn't, she just runs her hand gently over my weird shiny head. Her hand feels nice. Then she goes out of the room, crashing down the stairs and whooping. Sometimes, I guess, you just whoop to fill up all that empty air in the staircase. Maybe I'll try it sometime.

"Coming?" says Fish-boy, and I nod, taking one of the water bottles from where he's put them down on the edge of the tub.

"Coming," I say, handing him the other one.

We've only gone half a block when I remember something. "Hang on," I tell him. "I'll be right back." I mean to run, but I can't, so instead I slow jog back to the house and get my red Sharpie. Even the slow jog feels like a lot. Don't even get me started about how weird my scalp feels out in the air like that, the warm wind blowing on it like the breath of a crowd of giants.

I stick my pen in its regular pocket. I'm winded. I can feel my heart racing in response to the jog. It makes me feel like me, but also not like me. Me, with a naked head. Me, as an egg. Me, as a cancer patient. Me, as someone who gets winded jogging three hundred yards.

I jog back to Gavriel, and it's even harder going back. I'm sweating like mad. I can hardly breathe. My legs feel like noodles. I'm definitely not a machine.

"It's really cold on Mars," I tell Gavriel between gasps, and he nods.

"I bought a whole bunch of Mars books," he says. "I've read, like, half of them. Did you know there's a bookstore here where everything is fifty cents?"

"You went in there?" I say.

"Yeah," he says. "To buy books. Why? Is that weird?"

I shrug, "No," I say. Then I go, "Dad says it's not really a bookstore, it's a cover for a drug operation."

Gavriel bursts out laughing. "It's full of books!" he says. "The man behind the counter was about two hundred years old! He was really nice! He made me take extra books for free! Some of them are really dumb, though. They're from the 1980s. They were from before we knew anything about Mars at all, but people still thought they knew enough to write a whole book about it."

"Ha," I say. "I don't think Dad has ever actually been in that store." We keep walking, our feet making companionable stepping-sounds on the trail. "I used to like to imagine about Martians and stuff. Can I tell you something?"

He nods.

"Well, when the pictures started coming back of that rock that looked like it was floating, and the one that looked like a pyramid, and the one that looked like a woman, I still liked to imagine that there was a whole Martian thing that we just couldn't understand from here. Because we like to imagine everyone is like we are. And maybe that's their whole population: the woman, the floating rock, and the crab." I look at him. "You can laugh," I go. "It's lame, I know."

"It's …," he goes, shaking his head. "Really! I kind of think maybe Martians are just really tiny. Microscopic. We just think everything is going to be the same size and shape as us. Maybe they are so small we can't see them! Maybe they are studying us, and we're like giants or something. Big, kind of stupid giants."

I grin. "I thought that, too, for a while."

We are at the place where the path cuts down to the road for a bit. We walk by a few houses and then I say, "Wait a sec, hang on!" I jog-walk up to the "No Trespassers Aloud" sign on the Munros' old house and I fix it. A-L-L-O-W-E-D. Then I add a smiley face so that whoever owns the sign doesn't feel bad.

"You know that's my house, right?" he says, when I get back to him.

"It is?" I say. "I think I did know that. I just forgot." For a second, a clammy feeling comes over me. I *did* forget. What else have I forgotten? Is the Brussels sprout in there, just scrubbing away all my memories? I sit down on his lawn, which is dead, just like ours, and I cross my legs.

"What are you doing?" he says. "I'm not mad! It's kind of funny. I'm dyslexic. I can't spell anything."

"Oh," I say. "Now I feel bad."

He shrugs. "Don't feel bad," he says. "Dyslexic people usually grow up to own, like, Virgin Atlantic."

"Usually?" I say.

"Well, once," he admits. "That one guy."

"You probably will, too," I say.

"I don't want to!" he says. "I just want to be a doctor."

"Oh, right," I say. "I forgot." I take another breath. I'm forgetting more and more stuff! What if I forget the important things! What if when I thought about wiping my memory of all my Tig-related thoughts, it worked? Suddenly, I'm scared. I don't want to lose Tig!

"Just a minute," I say. I close my eyes. I try to remember the oldest thing that I can remember. I imagine going backward through time and picking up this memory and looking at it. I think about Christmases and birthdays and sitting on Santa's lap with Elliott when we were, like, two and four. I can remember that! We were wearing matching green dresses. In the picture, Elliott is pulling my hair and my face is all scrunched up like I'm going to scream. But am I remembering the actual time itself or just the picture?

I try to pick something else, something that there isn't a photo of. I try and try to think. I imagine the preschool, with all its finger paints and that weird goo the teacher would make with us. Then I've got it! I remember this one time that Tig decided to eat the goo. He started spooning it into his mouth like pudding. But then he choked on it. He couldn't breathe. I thought he was dead. He fell right over. His skin turned a funny cold bluish color, which was extra weird because his skin was usually this warm caramel. I walked over to him and said, "Bye-bye."

The teacher told Mom that I tried to put a blanket over his head. "I don't know how she knew to do that!" the teacher said, like Mom had maybe been showing me some footage of covering dead people with sheets instead of child-appropriate shows on PBS. Mom looked really embarrassed. I remember that, how ashamed she looked. Why didn't I give him the Heimlich? I just wrote him off! Of course, I was little. I didn't even know the Heimlich.

I open my eyes. *Tig,* I think. *I remember! It's OK.*

Gavriel plops down next to me. "Let me know when you're done," he goes.

"OK," I say. "I'm done. I was just trying to remember something."

"What were you trying to remember?" he says.

"Just something," I say, frustrated because it's hard to explain. "I was just trying to remember *something.*"

"OK, OK," he says, holding his hands up. "Jeez. Fine. Something. Whatever."

Gav gets up and holds out his hand to help me. I hesitate for a second before I take it, but then I do. We walk for a little bit without talking. My legs are wobbly, like I've been in bed for two months, which I sort of have been. I mean, I've been up. I just haven't really been going anywhere. I take a tiny tiny sip of water from Dad's bottle. It's nice and cold, so I take a bigger sip, but then I make myself stop. I don't want to throw up on Fish-boy's pink shoes. Why does everyone have pink shoes all of a sudden? Weird. Anyway, I'd hate for that to be my legacy. "Ish Love? Yeah, I knew her. She threw up on my shoes." No, thanks!

We cut across the road to where the trail that leads around the lake picks up again. The trail is at least a bit cooler. There are lots of big trees. Pines, mostly. They're, like, hundreds of years old. They are ancient. I think they've seen everything. A lot of people who have walked by these trees have died! Think about it. Now those watching, ancient trees have dropped their needles all over the path, like being without rain for so long is just making them give up. They throw long, spiky shadows over the dirt. With every step, we kick up clouds of dust. I think about how I always imagined kicking up clouds of dust on Mars. I think about whether I ever really thought I'd go. I think I did. Now I don't. I really don't. I know I won't. I put my hand to my eyes to see if I'm crying, but I'm not. I feel OK.

I kick the dirt extra hard and a huge cloud billows up from my foot and Gavriel sneezes.

"Why did you do that?" he says.

"I don't know," I say. "I sometimes do things now and I don't know why." I almost tell him about sprout Nirgal, Captain of the S.S. *My Brain*, but then I don't.

"Oh," he says. "That must be pretty weird."

"It scares me," I say, honestly.

"Oh," he says. He scratches his stomach in that way boys have, pulling his shirt to one side. I see a flash of his muscles.

"Do you work out?" I say. "Your stomach is muscly."

"Yeah," he says. "All the time. My dad left me his stuff. Well, he left his stuff. I mean, obviously he left it. He couldn't take it to … Sorry," he says. "I didn't think about you when I started to say that."

I stop walking and stare at him. His dad died from cancer. He told me that already, at the hospital, but I forgot and now I suddenly remember, which also makes me remember I'm going to die, too. I have cancer. It's pretty simple, I guess. A straighter line than you'd think. Like you imagine your life is this elaborate line that twists and curls and makes beautiful pictures, but the real beauty of life is that it isn't like that at all. It's a meteor, streaking across the sky. Meteors don't twist and turn. They just cut straight across, faster than you ever imagined. That's like life. A straight line. Someone should put that on a poster in the dentist's waiting room, probably, right next to that dead stars one.

"It's OK," I tell him. "I'm sorry about your dad." And it sort of is OK. I mean, it isn't. I don't want to die. But — and I'm sort of excited to think this — I'm going to be dead. I'm going to know what that's like. It's not quite like going to Mars, but it also is. Everyone wonders what it's like. No one is brave enough to go. "I'm pretty brave," I add.

"Yeah, totally," he says. "I've been thinking about Mars. I put in an application on that Mars Now site, but my mom says it's fake."

"Fake?" I go. "What do you mean?"

"She says she read somewhere that it was just a scam to get people to buy all the stuff, shirts and things. Hats. If you pay more, you get more points and then you get an acceptance, but it isn't real," he adds. He looks at me. My expression must have just changed to something like "shocked" or "horrified." He quickly adds, "But maybe it is! I mean, I don't know for sure! Don't look like that!"

"It's not real?" I say. "It's not." I feel a big emptiness opening up inside me. It's starting, I think. I don't feel scared. Maybe a little, I guess. I sit down on this fallen-over tree.

Gavriel sits down, too. He takes a few gulps of his water. Big, healthy gulps. *Glug, glug, glug.*

This one time, when I was little, we went to the Grand Canyon. We drove there. Everyone was fighting, so Dad had stopped at Best Buy and bought us each a cheap tablet. They were supposed to be like iPads but they weren't. They were really crummy. I was watching a movie on mine that I really liked. I think it was about golden retrievers in space. Anyway, we got to the viewing spot and Dad made us all get out of the car, and I was mad because I was watching my movie and Elliott just flat out refused because if she stopped the game she was playing, she'd lose all her points. "This matters more to me than you do!" she'd yelled at Dad. I guess it was the year after Disneyland. The terrible truth about the adoption was already out there.

I was still trying to always be good, at that point, trying to keep the peace. I put the movie down and I got out of the car and I stood beside Dad and there, in front of me, was this huge chasm. Obviously, the Grand Canyon is a hole, right? I hadn't really thought about what made it so beautiful. Just looking at it was so huge and great and everything. It was amazing. I hadn't realized! I mean, I was a kid. What did I know? But it wasn't the orange ground and the rock formations that were so astonishing to me. It was all the emptiness that all the other stuff was just a shell for. That's what I realized. I felt like the air whistled through me like music, like there was a pipe flute in my heart, playing something beautiful. That sounds corny, but it's true. I felt light. Like air.

On Mars, there's a canyon called Valles Marineris. It makes the Grand Canyon look like a crack in the sidewalk. It's so big, it's nothing but empty space. I think part of why I wanted to go to Mars was to see that. If the Grand Canyon made me feel like flute music, then the Valles Marineris would be that much more. It would be a whole symphony. My head throbs. I'm not ever going to see that Valles Marineris, I think, sadly.

"I don't feel good," I say, and even as I say it, I realize that something is really wrong, and then there's another crackle, just like the first one, but bigger. I'm the Earth — the Brussels sprout was right! — and this earthquake is the big one, the one that's going to destroy everything, the one that makes the tidal wave that wipes out the whole country, the whole planet, all of us, the one that's going to open up the canyon that cleaves the world in two.

I hit the ground hard. In the very far distance, I hear Gavriel yelling, "ISH ISH Ish Ish," but his voice is like a rock echoing when you throw it into the canyon and Elliott won't get out of the car and Mom and Dad are going to have a fight about it and Iris is standing there, silhouetted against the setting sun, looking like everything I wish that I was, and ISH and Ish and it doesn't matter, it's too late.

I can't go back.

22

It's different this time.

Mars, I mean. All of it. The glass is cracked all around the dome. The plants in the biome are wilted and dead. There's hardly any movement. Walking seems hard. Everything does. I sit in the dark and I look up through the glass to the place where I know the Earth is. I try to remember how colorful everything was, all the time. How we didn't have to work to make it bright, it just was. I try to remember why I wanted to come here so bad. Something in my head feels like it's alive, shifting slowly, and it hurts so bad. I can't stand it but I don't have a choice. I hold myself as still as I can. I'm sitting next to Gavriel and he's holding my hand. His eyes are closed. Everyone seems like they are barely breathing. I guess we aren't. We aren't because we aren't in suits and the glass is cracked, so we probably don't have any time. The radiation! The perchlorate! The carbon dioxide!

Tig is holding my other hand. No one is talking. I want them to say something, to tell me it's OK. I love them both so much, I feel like my insides are lit up with it. *I guess I love you*, I want to say. I've never felt like this. It's not like I want to kiss them, nothing like that. It's not like a crush kind of love. It's this whole other thing, I can't explain. It's belonging.

Beyond the glass, the stars are the same as they always are. I want to talk to them about dead stars, and about us, and about Mars and how we came here and then everything died and I guess we are going to, too. I'm not scared, not even a bit. I'm not scared because there isn't a choice. I'd be scared if I were swimming in the lake and I saw a crocodile seeing me and then slowly sinking under the surface. I'd be scared because I'd also think, "Maybe I can escape!" The cracked glass means that we can't escape. There is no choice here. Death is inevitable and that makes it not scary. Nothing can save us from this. I wonder what happened, but I can't ask, there's no one to ask.

Tig's and Gav's skin looks so white, it's glowing like light, and that's when I realize their hands are warm, too. Everything is glowing. I pull my hand away from Tig's and it's glowing, too. This is weird, I try to say. I miss my mom and dad and Iris and Elliott. I miss the house and the lake and Lunch Island. We didn't do our sleepover. I just wanted to do it once. Once would have been enough. I even miss the school, even though I only really went there for one day. I miss the hospital with the terrible art. But there isn't a reason to miss anything, because I suddenly figure out that it's all in me. It's all a part of me. I'm my own everything. I'm my own forever.

I'm a Universe of all things me. It makes sense. I'm a god. I'm God. We are all our own God. We are planets. We are canyons. We are striving to be beautiful. We are becoming empty space.

The boys look like glow sticks now. I want to tell them, but I can't. I know it's serious. Everything is serious. There are no jokes here, Dad, I want to say but can't. (Q: What do you call a mad cow? A: Mooooody.) I don't have a voice now because I'm a light. I'm light. I *am* light. Being light is easy. My skin is glowing and I'm not scared. I'm real because I figured out about love. It was at the last minute, but I still did it.

We are glowing more fiercely now, all three of us, we aren't just illuminated, we are illumination. It's pouring out of us, lighting up the dome with the dead and dying plants and I can see the remains of everything, of everyone else. Ashes and dust. It doesn't matter, they're gone.

We're shining so hard. We're burning.

Pretty soon now, it won't be long.

Then we'll burst out of this broken place, we'll float up there, we'll take our places where we belong, somewhere in the galaxy where we will be our own empty spaces. You won't be able to tell that we're dead yet, when you look. It takes light a long time to travel home.

I don't want to close my eyes, but I do. I close them and instead of it being dark, it's the opposite, it's like everything is the golden light of the sun dropping behind the hills and shining low across Lunch Island, turning it beautiful. It's like that but turned up, and I can see all kinds of stuff. I can see me and Tig in that tree house, trying to build a house of cards, the cards tipping and spilling every time one of us moved or giggled. I can see the bike ramp that we built in the woods, the way we rode down it over and over again until one or the other of us wiped out and started bleeding and the other one fainted. I can see Gavriel. My whole heart cracks open and the golden everything of what I feel is everywhere and then it's warm, suddenly, the right kind of warm and I know we're safe, we escaped, we're OK, it's over now. It's over and then there's not nothing, but not anything either, just a humming in between gold and warmth and love.

23

When I wake up this time, I know something is really different and really wrong. I'm cold. Totally freezing cold. Everything is blurry and gray. Something hard is digging into my side. There is a tube in my mouth and I can't talk. The strangest thing is that there are Christmas ornaments hanging on my IV pole. One is a Snoopy holding a bouquet of holly. The other one is a Rudolph with a broken, crooked leg. There's a big, pale blue star. My stuffed Ebola is perched at the top like the angel. I blink and blink. My eyes clear a little bit and then blur. I make a sound in my throat, it sounds like a cow, mooing. That's the punch line for something, I just can't remember what it is.

I'm in the hospital. It's a different room from last time. The painting on the wall is of some sheep in a field. It's pretty terrible. Hospital art must be universally terrible. Maybe they do that on purpose, so you'll want to leave. I know I must be alive because if I were dead, there wouldn't be a tube and I wouldn't hate that dumb picture so much.

I can't stop blinking. My eyes *tick tick tick*, just like

always. I hope someone hears them. I hope someone comes running over, but no one does. It must be night-time. It must be the middle of the night. I turn my head a bit and check the vinyl chair that's in the corner, like in all the rooms in this place, but it's empty and not the usual green, but instead, the blue of the sky when the sun has just set but it's not yet dark. I love that color but I hate that there is no one in the chair. That's not very nice, I think. That no one is sleeping here. Not even Mom.

My eyes are leaking. That happens. I must be sad. Lakes, lakes, lakes, everywhere. I'm having a hard time thinking. Each thought has to be knitted up somewhere by hand and then slowly passed along a chain of people until someone gives it to me and I try to figure out what it is. Is it a sock? No? It's a mitten?

I can't remember why I'm here. I have a Brussels sprout, steering this ship right into the path of danger. Nirgal, watch for meteors! I say. Maybe it's a whole stalk of sprouts now. I grew them in my greenhouse. The stalks would get so full they'd bend over from their own weight. I never saw them on Mars. Mars Now is not a lie! If it was, how could I have gone? The glass cracked. We all died. But at least we went. At least we tried. My head is itchy. I try to lift my hand to scratch, but my hand won't lift. Well, that sucks. Why is my hand so heavy? I try and I try and eventually I get my hand up and I give my skull a few good scratches. My skull has no hair! I have no hair! Then I remember how Elliott shaved my head. She's being so nice to me. Maybe she was nice all along. Maybe I just didn't notice because I was busy being mad at her. I went for a walk with Gavriel. Where is Gavriel?

Fish-boy, Fish-boy. He was nice, after all. He was OK. He told me that thing about the Velveteen Rabbit, which was important.

"ISH!" he said. I remember that. He's always shouting at me when I'm passing out, so I must have passed out. Was there a crackle? I try to remember, but I don't remember a crackle. It's really lonely in here. I mean, I've only been awake for five minutes and the loneliness is huge. It's like I've swallowed a lake of loneliness and it grew inside me and all that loneliness filled me up, like a jellyfish. No, it's not like that. Why am I thinking of jellyfish in the lake? I've never even seen one in there. I think they are in the sea. I've never gone swimming in the sea. I guess I won't now. It's too late for that.

They found running water on Mars. Maybe there is more of it. Maybe just under the cracks in the surface, there is even more and more. There's this lake some-where on Earth that is full of jellyfish. Not the stinging kind. You can swim with them. I bet on Mars, they have those. The jellyfish who don't sting. Maybe they will eat all the perchlorate. Maybe they will save the world. Well, not *the* world, but their own world.

After the spill in the lake, there weren't any fish, much less jellyfish. Those rainbow trout. All dead. Iris thinks the spill gave me the Brussels sprout. I never liked Brussels sprouts. No one does, except Mom. She cooks them up in the fry pan with bacon, which is a waste of good bacon, if you ask me.

Iris looked at all the kids in the chemo room and frowned. She said, "This is an awful lot of kids to have cancer in a small town."

And I told her, "They come from all over." The lake can't have given me cancer. I loved the lake. Lake Ochoa without the lake would just be Ochoa.

My tongue is super dry, but there is no water that I can see, plus this tube. I don't like it. I press my tongue against it and try to see if I can use my tongue to spit it out, but I can't. Once, I was eating a popsicle and it stuck to my tongue and I couldn't get it off. Tig had one, too, but his wouldn't stick. He tried to make it, but it just melted and then he ate it. He must have had a warm tongue. "Yourth ithn't thticky," I told him and we laughed and laughed, that popsicle just stuck there like a kid licking a frozen lamppost in a movie. Then he reached over and ripped it off and my tongue started bleeding and then he fainted.

Actually, that's not the best memory ever. I miss Tig but I think we're in a fight. I can't remember what it's about. Things don't have to be about so much, that's the truth. I'm like one of Mom's old people. "Where is my ride? I left the cookies in the oven!" I look at my hand to see if it's old, like maybe I'll see that I'm an old lady now and that's why I'm so confused, but my hand is the same as ever. It looks silver in the shadowy light in this room. Silver is so cold. I don't think I like it. It's like you can be a dog person or a cat person, a gold person or a silver one. I'm a gold. We never had pets, except Buzz Aldrin. Some people are bird people. I think I let him go. I think he flew and I didn't follow him. Things that fly: Parrots. Butterflies. Moths. Stars.

It's like I can almost remember something important, but the memory keeps slipping away; the more I try to get to it, the further it goes. I fall asleep trying. I dream about Mars again. In the dream, we are rebuilding something. It's hard work. Everything is heavy and cold and impossible. But I keep doing it. I lift things and hold them in place. Tig is there and so is Gavriel. We build and build. The dream is tiring. At the end, we go inside and we look around and there's this huge pool.

"This can't be," I say through the blurry dream. "There's no water like this on Mars."

"It's just a dream," says Tig. "We already died." He looks happy when he says it, but also sad.

"You said you'd never leave me alone, and then you did," I say. I'm mad.

"Get over it," he says. "Everyone messes up. You, too."

"I did, a lot," I say.

Then suddenly I notice people in the pool. It's all the kids from my class! They are wearing sparkly bathing suits. They are swimming like synchronized swimmers in the Olympics, these fake grins plastered on their faces, the water splashing all around. I start to cry, watching them.

"What's wrong?" Tig says. The light shines off his bald head.

"Leave her alone," says Fish-boy, who is also bald. "Don't you get it?"

"No," says Tig. "I don't."

"I do," says Fish-boy. "She's my friend, too." He puts his hand over my hand and squeezes it.

I'm relieved because I don't have to explain to him how the synchronized swimmers make the dream so clearly a dream. We already said good-bye to Mars. My last Mars dream was the final one. This is just one of those normal ones like everyone has: a compilation dream. In the dream, Mr. Wall strolls into the room and shouts, "POP QUIZ!" I haven't studied. I laugh. The clock hands spin backward. A bunch of tiny purple Martians run by, twirling and laughing, like a punctuation mark at the end of the story that was my dream of Mars. It's not real, not Mars, not a vision of the future or anything like that, just my brain making a pattern of memories and twisting them up into something that's a lie. It's not ever going to happen, after all. I mean, it's a lot to convey through a hand squeeze inside a dream, but it's still pretty nice, to feel understood.

I wake up crying, choking on the pipe in my throat. I might be laughing. I can't tell.

"Ish!" Dad says, and he's beside me, hugging me and saying things that are too fast for me to understand.

On Mars, we learn to talk slowly. There's probably a reason, but I don't know what it is. Brain mush or something that happened on the trip, our bones melting away into our brains.

I try to tell him to slow down but there's a tube in my mouth so I squint my eyes. I try to tell him with my eyes. He's talking and talking about a seizure and a coma and new medicine and I'm going to be OK. It's just that the Brussels sprout is now a cabbage, but a small one, and does my head hurt?

Yes, it really does, Dad, I want to say, it's bad. But I can't. I'm so sleepy. It shouldn't work this way, I think, and then I fall asleep again and when I wake up the person next to my bed isn't Mom or Dad or Iris or even Elliott, it's Tig, and he's bald. I blink and blink. *Slish, slosh, slish*. Either my dream is leaking out my eyes or this isn't real.

"Oomf," I say, because I can't talk. I mean, "I waited, like you said."

"Hey," he says. He looks really uncomfortable.

Well, I can't blame him. I want to say, "Don't faint," but I can't.

His eyes slide off the IV needles in my hand, the tube in my mouth, and finally land on the window.

"Mom finally drove me down," he says. "I'd been asking and asking and asking and finally she did. I was super mad. I was like, she's going to die!" He stops himself. "I mean, I didn't want it to be too late." He holds his hands out and inspects them. I don't know what he's looking for. Maybe just to make sure he's still the same as always, even though I'm not. "It's weird here now," he goes. "Like everything is smaller. The park benches and everything."

I nod. When I look at his face, even though it's blurryish, I see everything we ever did together. That time we thought it sounded like fun to climb up onto the roof to look at the stars but the roof was sloped and we both slid right off and he broke his arm. Mom and Dad were so mad at us. The go-kart race we entered in third grade and our go-kart broke on the starting line, the wheels just splaying out like it couldn't even stand the idea of our combined weight. The time he spat on Kaitlyn's hair when she was mean to me and then pretended he hadn't done it. All those Mars Now applications. The ones we filled out with fake names (who didn't get accepted, either). The way we thought it was real. He thinks everything looks smaller, but I think everything looks younger. He looks really young. He's a kid. I'm so confused. He's just a kid. We're both kids. Why do I feel so old?

We've only been on this planet for thirteen years. That's not very long when you think about forever. It's a blip. We're blips. We're still in the early stages.

He goes, "I went to the tree house and it's gone. Like it crashed, completely." He makes a *crash* sound with his mouth somehow. "Um, you probably knew that." He shrugs. "I found this." He puts my old copy of *The Martian* on my chest. It's all torn up. It smells like mold and water. It's been raining. It must have rained.

I've missed the rain. I wonder if the lake filled back up, if he'll go to Lunch Island, and I try to blink the questions but he just shifts back and forth from one foot to the other. I can tell that talking to me while I'm not answering is making him struggle for words. "It's like email!" I want to tell him. "I'll answer later!"

"I gotta go," he says, and then really fast, so fast that if I blinked, I'd miss it, he leans over and kisses me on the forehead. "I shaved my head for you," he adds. "I don't have cancer or anything."

"Thanks," I want to say.

I want to tell him what I know about love, but suddenly I don't remember and I don't know and then I'm asleep again.

This time, there's just a space. This time, there isn't dreaming. I try really hard, but I don't hear any music.

Not yet.

24

I sleep and wake up and there are people and then there aren't. Mom is saying something. What is she saying? "And comma hast thou slain the Jabberwock question mark carriage return Come to my arms comma my beamish boy exclamation mark carriage return O frabjous day exclamation mark Callooh exclamation mark Callay exclamation mark carriage return He chortled in his joy period." He chortled in his joy period, I think. That's funny!

Sometimes I'm not sure if I'm imagining the people or not. One time, I open my eyes and Camilla and Zoe are there, just staring at me and crying. Another time, it's Buzz Aldrin (the astronaut, not the parrot) and he's crying, too. So much crying! I want to say no. I want to explain, "It's the joy period!" I want to tell them that it's OK, but it really isn't, so I don't. Elliott sits in the vinyl chair and throws my stuffed Ebola up and down. When it spins, it leaves a rainbow trail in the air and I want to say, "Look, did you see that?" It's all in slow-motion and then it speeds up. There are doctors and nurses. People use flashlights to look into my eyes. I'm dying. The Brussels sprout won and I lost, but isn't it just a part of me, it's a part of everything. It makes sense to me and then it doesn't. It's as big as a cabbage now. Have you ever looked closely at a cabbage? Those leaves have these beautiful patterns. They are the same as a bee's wings. Those lines tracing through them, I mean. The cabbage blooms and blooms and blooms like one of those animated gifs, growing forever leafier, filling me up with leafiness.

Everything is just elements, jumbled together, old stars trying to make themselves into something else, even if it's just for a minute, even if it's for twelve years. I mean, thirteen.

Fish-boy reads out loud from *The Martian*. It's so unrealistic! I want to say. He never mentions the perchlorate problem! I want to tell him not to go now. The glass will break. I don't know what is true. The dreams come crowding in when I'm awake, and I'm scared because I can't tell the difference.

Gavriel's mom touches my forehead like she knows me, and her hands are smooth and cool. Paging Dr. Klein. The truth is, I've forgotten everything except this joke: Q: Have you heard about the first cow to go into space? A: He landed on the moooooon. It's funny to me. Oh, I'm funny. Me! Funny! I'm not so hard-edged as everyone thought. I'm not so serious. I wish I'd bought that sparkly sweater. I should have had pink shoes.

Dad's there in the chair sipping water out of the water

bottle. Some of us are stars but some of us are water. He's the good kind. Golden, warm, and welcoming. Dive in. I'll miss the lake. I miss Buzz Aldrin. Just as I think that, he flies by the window outside, glowing like a moon, in slow motion. I can feel his feathers pushing down the air. I miss my laptop, even though it didn't curl up and purr. I miss the way the light filtered through the trees and made long rays of sun that Fish-boy and I walked through that day on the path. "God's fingers" he called them, and I hope he's right, I hope there's a God and he held us in his hand, just for that minute we passed through. I don't think it's God, necessarily. I think it's Everything. That's what love looks like, I guess. I guess I love you. We walked through it and now I'm going to go into it again but this time alone, but it's OK. I like being alone. It's good for my Mars Now application for them to know that, in case everyone else doesn't make it. They have to know that I'll be OK. I'll just keep going, planting things and waiting for everyone else to come. I'll have potatoes to feed them. Maybe even Brussels sprouts.

"Oh," they'll say, "you were so brave to go first!" and I'll nod and say, "I totally was!" and they'll tell me about all the lists that I'm on, the way everyone remembers me. And anyway everywhere everywhere everywhere the golden light. Look at it. It's right here. It's in the room. It's in me.

It's raining, too. Pouring. It's filling up the room. It's

overflowing in my eyes. It's the kind of rain that fills empty lakes, that fills everything, sloshing back and forth in a bathtub, overflowing. Clean rain. It's lashing against the glass in huge prisms, pink and silver. I think it's a miracle. It's finally a miracle. I'd been waiting and then it just came, it just happened. Look! Can't you hear how beautiful it is? A symphony, a whole symphony, playing everywhere, playing inside me, singing about all my beautiful forevers.

Acknowledgements

To everyone at Algonquin Books for Young Readers for believing in my vision for this book, for trusting me to make it happen and for letting it go where few middle grade books have gone before, thank you! I feel so incredibly lucky to see my books in your catalogue. Krestyna, Elise, Eileen, Sarah, Brunson, Trevor, Brooke, Judit, Lauren and all my author-siblings: You make me feel like I belong, and I am so grateful that my books are at home here.

To my Canadian publishers at Dancing Cat Books for promoting and sharing my book in my home country, thank you, too!

I owe a huge debt to Andy Weir and his wonderful, information-laden novel, *The Martian*. I don't generally read science fiction, but people kept encouraging me to read his book. Finally I relented and read it and I knew, instantly, that *this* is the book that Ish would have devoured, absorbing and rearranging the facts as she saw fit. It is exactly the kind of "adult" fiction that anyone from a middle-grader (although not the intended audience!) to an adult would love: densely packed with facts, full of action, and so compelling. It's the exact book that I would have taken from my dad's bookshelf at 11 or 12 and read under the covers with a flashlight. I needed for Ish to have a fulcrum to hang her fantasies on and *The Martian* became that, to her. So thank you Andy Weir for writing exactly the right book at the right time for Mischa Love to fall in love with, for inspiring her (and me) to learn more and to find our own version of Mars, cobbled together with facts, fantasy, and our imaginations.

There are so many scientists, astronomers, researchers, organizations, and authors who unknowingly helped me. I couldn't name them all if I tried, but I so appreciate them for doing the hard work of analyzing the facts, for presenting information in an understandable way, for continuing to research a future settlement on Mars, in spite of the fact that so many people think it's just a pipe dream. The information is everywhere and the Internet is full of resources (sometimes accurate, sometimes conflicting, but always interesting).

This book also would not exist without the help I received from so many other people. The late Sumant Krishnaswamy, who answered my most elementary questions when I first began; my friends who let me think-out-loud and work out plot points over drinks, coffee, and on long woodsy-walks; my incredibly supportive and knowledgeable writers' group; and, last but not least, to my amazing agent, Jennifer Laughran — thank you, thank you, thank you!

And, of course, to my readers. I am most of all grateful for you! Let me know what you thought of Ish's story. You can find me on the internet at www.karenrivers. com. I love hearing from you! Thank you for reading my book. I hope you liked it.